EYNHALLOW

Tim McGregor

**RAW DOG
SCREAMING
PRESS**

Published by Raw Dog Screaming Press
Bowie, MD

First Edition

Cover: Illustration Nerves of the hand. | Traité complet de
l'anatomie de l'homme comprenant la medecine operatoire, by
Jean-Baptiste Marc Bourgery and illustrated by Nicolas-Henri Jacob
Thomas Fisher Rare Book Library, University of Toronto.
Cover Layout: Tim McGregor
Interior Layout: Jennifer Barnes

Printed in the United States of America

This is a work of fiction. Any resemblance to persons
living or dead is unintentional.

ISBN: 978-1-947879-66-9 / 978-1-947879-67-6
Library of Congress Control Number: 2023948868

RawDogScreaming.com

Also by Tim McGregor

Wasps in the Ice Cream

Taboo in Four Colors

Lure

Hearts Strange and Dreadful

The Spookshow series (books 1-11)

Just Like Jesse James

Old Flames, Burned Hands

Killing Down the Roman Line

Bad Wolf trilogy

To my two monsters, Ruby and Ginger

EYNHALLOW

The last inhabitants of Eynhallow abandoned the island in 1841. The remaining domiciles were destroyed a decade later to prevent future habitation. The island is off limits to all visitors, save for one designated day of the year.

ORKNEY ISLANDS

August 30th, Year of our Lord, 1797

It is dark, but it is not quiet. The wind never stops here, nagging the shutters or rattling the door like it wants to come in. The breath of God, some call it. Not me, but others. Rain pummels the roof and leaks through the thatch. A summer storm passing over our island. The racket is enough to raise the dead, but not loud enough to wake the children. I know all of their individual snores and the brood sleeps through it all. Thankfully, there is no thunder.

I am envious. Is there anything more vexing than being bone tired but unable to sleep? The bed is comfortable enough and Lord knows how weary I am, but my thoughts scamper away like a mouse through a pantry. I want the comfort of oblivion, of peace, but concerns over the children or the house, the squalor we endure, nag me relentlessly. Sleep is a shy pony. I cannot entice it to eat from my hand.

Shush now, Agnes. All of it can wait till the morrow because Lord knows the morning will come soon enough and then where will you be? Stupid woman. Sleep. I set out every pot and receptacle I possess to catch the rainwater, but now the drip-drip-drip is one more distraction. I wonder if death is really so bad or if it is simply a way to catch up on all the sleep one misses in a lifetime? Saints in a rowboat, listen to me. I am delirious from fatigue.

A hand in the darkness. It lands on my hip, kneading the tip of bone through my nightdress. If my eyes were open, they would roll over in umbrage. He squirms up next to me, the hand moving along, getting to the point.

"Not now," I whisper. "I'm tired."

His voice is sloppy with drink and neediness. "It's been ages, Agnes. Please."

How I hate his pleading tone in moments like this. Mr. Tulloch is prone to gruffing out orders and demands. Hearing it shift into a whinge is as grating as it is unwelcome.

"Let me sleep," I tell him. "Go on now. Back to your side of the bed."

This only makes him badger me more. He paws at me and pleads, argues, and insists. It is his right, he says. He's had a hard day and wants a moment's pleasure.

"Is that so much to ask for?" he adds. "Come now. Be a good girl."

He won't stop, not when he's had his tipple and his pole is bumping my hip. So, I relent. I hike up my nightdress because I don't want him tearing it. It has enough holes as it is. He rolls onto me. It's too dark to see his face, but I can smell his grin.

My palm flattens against his chest, halting his approach. "You cannot spill inside me," I warn him. "You understand? I mean it, Robert."

"Agnes, that spoils the whole thing," he whines. "You know this."

I push him back. I am quite strong, you know. Much stronger than my husband. I draw my line in the sand.

"Promise me you'll pull short. I want no more babies."

He agrees with a sloppy sincerity, eager to get on with it. I stop him again.

"Promise me or go without."

He sighs and promises and promises.

I withdraw my hand. "You said that last time," I remind him. "And you did it anyway."

"My mistake," he says, and almost sounds contrite. "Come on now. Let us in. There's a good girl."

"Don't say that."

"Hush now."

There is a gap of years between us, but not enough for that kind of talk. I find it unpleasant. How much of a gap? Mr. Tulloch is three and forty years. I am nine and twenty. Or is it thirty now? My mind goes to silly places while he has his way.

I'm not paying attention, missing the cues I should be minding. He picks up the pace and his grunting grows louder. His "sweet words" become vile.

"Robert, stop. Get off, damn it!"

He only gallops faster, his hands pinning my arms. I push him off, squirm back and my greedy husband spills over my thighs. Did I retreat fast enough? Please, God, no. No more babies. I am tired.

My snarl is sharp. "Damn it, Robert. You promised!"

"Shh," he says. "You'll wake the children."

I hiss like a cornered cat. "Is it asking too much? To honor a promise rather than being so bloody selfish?"

8

"I'm sorry, love," he groans. "I get carried away. It's your comeliness that does me in. How can I resist?"

I wipe his mess off me. I have half a notion to rub it in his smug face.

"So, it's my fault, is it?"

His chuckle is a loose and rattling thing, like pebbles shaken in a cup. He rolls onto his side of the bed, sighs, and promptly falls asleep.

How does he do it? He just closes his eyes and drops immediately into slumber, where I must cool my thoughts with hard effort just to entice sleep. It isn't fair.

Fair. Listen to me. What in life is fair? Not a speck.

But now I am awake, while Mr. Tulloch slumbers like the dead. Not only am I awake, I am flushed from the tumbling. Well. I know one way that will cool my thoughts and ease the tension in my jaw. A moment's play, quiet and under the covers. Then I, too, will sleep like the dead.

A cry in the night ruins everything. Our youngest is sobbing again. She's often unwell, our little Effie. Sickly since the day she was born. I get out of bed and pad across the cold floor to quiet her. I wonder what the hour is and how soon before the sun rises on our Holy Isle?

CHAPTER I

Four children and one small house does not make for a placid home. Walls of undressed stone and a roof of smoked thatch. Two rooms. A generation ago, as Mr. Tulloch tells it, half the house was a barn where his family wintered the sheep and cows. You can still smell them, their musk is seeped into the stone and the timber beams. If I complain about it, Mr. Tulloch tells me that it is the smell of bygone prosperity. If that is the case, I can only imagine that squalor smells like summer roses.

Effie is doing poorly after a rough night. A tiny mite of a thing with her father's eyes and my unruly hair. She is four years old, the baby of the brood. Her croup has gotten worse, and her nose is a rouge button. Her older sister, Grace, rubs her back and tries to get her to drink a little goat milk.

"No milk, Grace," I tell my eldest. "It'll make the cough worse. Just water."

"Yes, ma'am."

Grace is twelve and practically a second right hand to me. As the oldest of the four, she helps look after her siblings. She helps with everything, in fact. What would I do without her? I need to tell her that. Tell her how important and special she is to me. But there never seems a proper time and on the rare occasion that I attempt to express it, Grace just turns red at my clumsy words. She's grown up so fast, it astonishes me.

A nudge at my rump interrupts my thoughts, followed by a harsh bleating. Someone has let the goat inside. Again.

"Meg, take that animal outside where it belongs."

Her name is Margaret, but she will not answer to that name. Meg it is then. She is a bit of the black sheep here in the Tulloch household. The only red in a family of chestnuts. She spits like an old Orkneyman and punches her brother for no reason.

Meg lifts her freckled face to me. "But, Daisy wants her breakfast too."

The goat has the temerity to bleat at me again, pleading her case. My finger points to the door.

10

"Out."

I see Meg curse under her breath. I've stopped scolding her to be a little lady, because there is nothing remotely ladylike about our second daughter. The child throws a leg over Daisy and rides the smelly goat out the door. She manages to stay on for a dozen paces before tumbling into a puddle. She squeals in delight.

Lord above, how have I failed my own children so terribly?

Kit hovers near me as I stir the cauldron, bowl in hand and at the ready. The boy is forever famished, no matter how much he stuffs into his mouth.

"Is it ready now?" he wants to know. "It looks ready. It smells ready. It must be ready."

He holds out his bowl. The gruel in the cauldron is not cooked through yet, but I ladle a portion in his bowl just to keep him quiet. He'll still be hungry when the porridge sets. Like his sister, Christopher does not like his Christian name, so we call him Kit. He considers it the perfect name, but his sister disagrees. Meg calls him Kitten just to annoy him and make him chase her round the croft. If I am not careful, one of these two will murder the other. And I do not want any more dead babes. I have had my fill of those, thank you very much.

Effie sniffles from her perch, her eyes puffy and pink. When the porridge is ready, her bowl is the first to be filled. The poor thing needs her strength to ward off any of the countless ailments she suffers from. My cupboard holds precious little sugar, but I sneak a pinch into her bowl to make sure she eats it all. Unlike her brother, Euphemia is never hungry. God only knows what sustains her because she eats like a bird.

Her small hands cup the bowl for warmth and those big penny eyes meet mine. "Is Father not having breakfast with us?"

"He'll sup when he returns," I tell her. "Now eat up, darling. I want to see that bowl spotless, yes?"

"I'll finish hers if she doesn't want it," her brother chimes in. You'd think the lad's never been fed before.

I tell him to mind his own meal for now and ladle out the rest of the gruel. Equal shares all round. Meg complains about Kit having two helpings to which the boy responds by calling his sister goat-face.

"No more talk," I reprimand. "Eat."

Mr. Tulloch was up and out the door at first light after a restful night's sleep. How wonderful for him. I am still irked at his selfish tumbling, and more than a little on edge about the consequences. Did I push him off in time? The thought of being with child again is repugnant. How on earth could I corral four savage children with swollen feet and an aching back? How would I eat for two when there's barely enough for one? To say nothing of the heartbreak if the child is born blue or expires shortly afterward. Three times now I have held cold baby flesh that will not warm no matter how I rub it by the fire. I will murder Robert if there is one nesting in my belly now.

Our cramped home holds but one mirror, a delicate oval of looking glass within an ornate frame. It belonged to my mother. The only heirloom of hers that I was allowed to take. It hangs from a nail in the west wall, but I barely recognize the woman in it now. Who is this person with crow's feet and a wan complexion?

Agnes Eliza Tulloch, née Burness. My hair is common brown, my eyes copper. My hands are calloused and big enough to close around a man's skull. By the standard used to measure horses, I stand nineteen hands in height. Outlandishly tall with unwomanly strength and an inordinate tolerance for pain. My backbone may not be the straightest, but it is as sturdy as oak. More tree than maiden, my stepmother used to titter. The witch.

The children prattle quietly over their breakfast. Kit has devoured his and is already watching for anyone who doesn't finish theirs. I am granted a moment's peace, until Effie squeals. Something has fallen into her bowl. Meg hoots with laughter as I follow the children's gaze to the ceiling.

A spark of sunlight twinkles through the thatch. Twigs rain down on our breakfast table, causing the children to cover their bowls. Effie refuses to eat, saying her porridge is ruined. Kit immediately volunteers to lap it up, twigs, and all.

"Look," says Grace. "We have a visitor."

The hole in the thatch rattles and shakes, causing more debris to fall. A gull pokes its head through to blink at us. Then it goes back to pecking at our roof.

The children become excitable again. Last night's storm has damaged an already compromised roof. I told Mr. Tulloch it needed patching, to which he huffed impatiently and said he would see to it. Now this stupid bird has found a chink and is laying siege from above.

I shout at the thing to clear off, but the gull just pecks away. Standing on the bench, I almost snatch it by the neck, but it flaps away. I do what I can to patch the hole from this side, squishing and threading the reeds into place.

"Mam's a giant," says Effie.

"Giantess," corrects her brother.

"Don't say that," Grace scolds. "Eat your breakfast."

Grace, bless her heart, knows I can be overly sensitive about my height. I've been called worse, believe me, and I know there is no malice in what the children say. On occasion though, my height comes in handy. The breach is patched, and everyone goes back to their meal. Kit hovers over the pot at the hearth, scraping up what was supposed to be my own breakfast. Well then, I shall have to content myself with black tea. The day's work needs doing.

CHAPTER II

The storm has left the island wet and sopping, but the morning is bright and blue. The wind, which normally blows brisk, is reduced to a gentle waft. There is no escape from the wind on Eynhallow. It never ceases, even on gentle summer days. Its never-ending whistle almost drove me mad during my first year on the island. I barely notice it now. Summer storms means wrack, and wrack means kelp that can be harvested, so I gather up our baskets and march my brood out across the heath to the southern shoreline. Grace kneels to let Effie climb onto her back while Meg challenges her brother to a race. Daisy, the goat, follows at a distance. The smelly thing is more dog than bovine, as it rarely lets Meg out of her sight.

The trek to the beach is not far, through the ankle-high heather and past the Kemp cottage where my friend, Katie, lives. Eynhallow is one of the smaller isles in the Orkneys, its defining characteristics much the same as the others. Heath and peat at its core, shale cliffs and a pebbly beach where it meets the sea. It is as desolate or bountiful as one's imagination, I suppose. Not an easy life here. The constant wind dries the eyes and salty spray coarsens the flesh. Mr. Tulloch is fond of saying that the island is as plentiful as one is willing to make it. "It toughens the soul," he likes to admonish should I ever complain about the conditions. Or the squalor or the starvation or lack of respect. My nerves are still a bit flinty from lack of sleep.

One must be born on Eynhallow to be considered a true islander. My husband is one, I am not. They sometimes speak their own patois here, these native Eynhallow people. A coarse-sounding sort of cluck and lilt that confounds me or is used in whisper behind my back. Being an off-islander is one thing, you see. Being a giantess, well, that is a whole other cloth that wags tongues and gapes eyeballs. It no longer bothers me. I've lived with it since my thirteenth year, when a tortuous growth spurt stretched these bones to their unmaidenly length. Mr. Tulloch is three inches stacked onto five feet. I tower a full head and shoulders over him, which makes for an odd couple, I admit. I was on my knees when our vows were made, and still the groom insisted on standing on an apple crate.

Effie, perched like a monkey on Grace's back, directs her sister as one does a horse to draw up alongside me so that we walk together. The babe likes to prattle as much as her sisters, often peppering me with questions. Most of them silly but delivered with all the gravitas that a four-year-old can muster.

"Will there be a shipwreck? Or maybe a whale stranded on the shore? How will we roll it back out to sea? Not even you're that strong, Mam."

"Who knows what we'll find, pet," I reply. "Maybe we'll find a stranded mermaid?"

Grace snorts a laugh. At twelve, she is long past the talk of fairies and island trolls. "All we're going to find is seaweed. Maybe a few stinking fish."

Effie claps her hands. "What if we find one of the finfolk? It is summer. Don't they come ashore during summer to steal children?"

"They're said to come ashore when it's warm," I tell her. "But they do not take children. What would they want with a babe?"

"For supper," the child answers without hesitation.

"They don't eat children, Effie. They're sea spirits. They eat only fish."

I believe this is her brother's handiwork at play. Kit loves to scare his sisters with ghost stories. Grace has no patience for his nonsense and Meg tends to kick him when he tries to be mean. Effie, on the other hand, eats up her brother's stories like honeyed oatmeal. I'll need to remind Kit not to scare his youngest sister.

Mind you, there is no lack of ghost tales or sprite stories on the island. From what I've been told, Eynhallow means 'holy isle.' Most likely that name is due to the ruins on the southern bend; an old monastery or church from the middle ages, but it also may refer to the strange Norse spirits said to haunt the place. The finfolk are some sort of fish creatures who take on a human appearance when they crawl up the beach. Or there are the trolls who dwell on the rocky Bowcheek end. They hide in the cliff caves during the day and skulk about the island at night looking for something to feast on. There is also the abandoned cottage on the north end, near the ancient standing stones. It is said to be haunted by a restless ghost. No wonder Effie worries about goblins and monsters. The island is rife with them.

Over a small rise and we are here. The beach is rich with dark heaps of kelp, plucked by the storm and tossed ashore. Nature provides, but sometimes it rains plenty. Everyone in our small troop takes a basket and begins collecting the tentacled mass of seaweed. Boiled and salted, dulse will make for a sturdy meal if one is hungry enough. Practical too, as it can be dried and hung for long periods until needed on winter nights when the larder is bare. All up and down the beach, the wrack of kelp glistens in the sun. There is so much of it that most of our day will be spent gathering and hauling it back to the croft. There is enough here even to burn for potash, which we can sell to soap makers and glass blowers on the mainland. A few precious shillings to add to our paltry purse.

Back and forth we trudge with our baskets, dumping the slick stuff into a heap outside the cottage door. Passing the Kemp cottage on my way back to the beach, I spot Katie sitting in the sunshine, shelling peas. I wave and she waves back. Katie Kemp is kind and sweet, but she is also, behind closed doors, quite funny and often bawdy. She is very dear to me, because without Katie's kind ear, I would have gone mad long ago. I watch her get up, wave again to me, and then waddle inside. Katie is very, very with child. Her seventh. If it survives, of course. I don't expect it will trouble her. All of Katie's children came into the world with a minimum of fuss. I should know, as I've attended all but one.

The serene day lasts, making our chore pleasant, but by late afternoon we are all somewhat spent. The children have grown bored and are taking turns riding Daisy. So far, only Meg has mastered the art of hanging on for a dozen paces before the animal bucks her off. Even Grace gives it a try, which makes me happy. She's become such a serious little lady. It's nice to hear her laugh.

My weariness gets the better of me and I lay the basket aside to sit and look out at the sea. I love the water. The swells cast a spell and the sound of the surf calms every nerve. Some nights, when my brains are too crazed and the weather permits, I come down here to sleep on the beach. Those nights I sleep the deepest. Or I wake up drenched when the heavens suddenly erupt and wash away my rest. I rarely get sick or catch cold, though. Soaked to the skin and chilled to the bone, it doesn't seem to bring on fevers or shivering the way it does in others. My father claimed it was a superior constitution, inherited from himself, of course. My stepmother took offense at it, saying it was strange and unnatural. I don't remember what my mother made of it. She died when I was seven, giving birth to my brother, who also died. They were buried together. I used to visit their grave when I was younger, but it has been a long time since I have been back to Kirkwall. I miss it sometimes. Not just my mother's grave, but the town itself. There are streets there. With shops and people walking about, and even a bakery.

The population of Eynhallow totals twenty souls. Four families in all. Needless to say, it can be lonely.

CHAPTER III

A tug on my sleeve, interrupting me. "Mother, it's late. We need to go home."

Grace's voice is like a pinch to the flesh. The tide is coming in and the horizon is painted pink. Grace is at my side, saying it is time to go.

Pebbles slur underfoot as I stand, foggy-headed and unsteady. I've done it again.

She looks annoyed with me. "Are you all right?"

"Yes, yes. Let's get on then."

The other children look terribly bored, and I shoo them on toward home. I hate when I do this—woolgather into oblivion by the shore. I've let the day slip away from me and now the children are cold, and supper will be late. I lift Effie onto my hip and hurry the others along impatiently like it is their fault we are late and not mine. If luck is with me, Mr. Tulloch hasn't returned home to wonder where his family is. But I have never been a lucky person.

He's there, sitting at the table when we tumble through the door like geese.

"Well, there you are," my husband announces. The grin on his face is unpleasant. "Here I thought the lot of you had been snatched by trolls, leaving me with a cold kitchen."

"It is my fault," I confess. "I lost track of the time."

"Do tell," he says dryly. My husband often delights in other people's mistakes, making hay of small things. I don't know why.

Mr. Tulloch is every inch an Orkneyman. Strong hands calloused from toil and a countenance etched from the never-ending wind. His jacket is well made, but old, with elbows patched more than once by my needle and thread. The battered cap, which he rarely takes off even indoors, is always tilted at a jaunty angle. He believes this gives him a youthful appearance, one of high spirits and mirth, but perceptions can be slippery things. He is quick with a sharp word, and even quicker with a sharp hand if slighted. He enjoys being right.

The long-stemmed pipe is porcelain and belonged to his father. He lights it now, one eye peering over the flame at his errant family.

"The meal is delightful, by the way," he says. The table before him is bare. "You've really outdone yourself, my dear."

Grace has always been overly sensitive to any acrimony between us. She winces. I believe it physically pains her to hear us squabble. "We gathered so much kelp today, Father," she says. "Did you see it piled outside?"

How awful does one have to be for their child to make excuses? I should be ashamed, but contrition eludes me when I see the rosy blooms on Mr. Tulloch's cheeks. He's had his snout in the spirits, of course. There is nothing to be done about my tardiness, so I simply rush to get something on the table. Yesterday's broth and a heel of bread that I'll have to divvy up between the five of them.

"Aye, the kelp," he says through the pipe vapor. "A great harvest of it, I see."

"The shore was piled with the stuff, Father," adds Kit. Like his sister, the boy dislikes tension between his parents and often tries to distract one of us from it. "We gathered enough to burn for the ash."

Meg is still too young to detect the flintiness between us. She blurts everything out. "Mother got distracted by the water."

A blade to the back. An innocent statement, but it stings all the same.

"Again?" her father asks. "The sea holds some strange enchantment for your mother, doesn't it?"

"Go wash up now." I shoo the children on and get to work. I can feel my husband's gaze on me like a hot coal to the flesh.

He puffs on the pipe. "You're woolgathering is becoming a real problem, isn't it?"

"Nothing so dramatic as that, Robert."

He sneers at this. "It'll be the death of you yet, staring out to sea like that. Or the death of one of the wee ones."

The pot slams onto the board. "Let's not get carried away."

"What if one of them slipped into the water while you're under a spell?" He waves the pipe over the empty table. "Today it's dinner, tomorrow it might be a drowned child."

He's in a mood and there's little to be done to turn the conversation around. Mr. Tulloch often works with Mr. Heddle, down the way. The two of them conclude their workday with a glass of the peat whiskey that Mr. Heddle distills himself. Robert returns home red-cheeked and chatty, eager to indulge his favorite hobby of picking at my many flaws. He tells me it is for my own education and betterment. How else will I ever learn? I thank him for this kindness by not poking his eye out with the spoon.

I grit my teeth and hurry the meal as he prattles on. I am still vexed at him for his selfishness last night and his education of my character is brewing a bitter soup this night. I take it out by banging the pot and chopping the knife hastily, but I am careless and pay for it with a cut to my thumb. It is deep and blood spills all over the diced turnip. Stupidly, I cry. Not at the pain, but the frustration coiled inside my chest. It all comes blubbering out.

"Good Lord," Mr. Tulloch exclaims. In a flash he is on his feet and helping me. He squeezes a cloth over my hand to staunch the blood and rips another into strips. Within moments he has the wound bandaged and the hand elevated above my head. A trick he learned from his father, also a fisherman.

"There, there," he says, wiping a tear from my cheek. "Sit tight now. Grace will get supper on."

How this man can spin his face about is beyond me. Cruel one minute, then kind and sweet the next. I sit like a block of wood with my hand in the air, watching my daughter warm the broth and my husband set the table. Why can't he be consistent? Keep the kind face and leave the cruel one outside with the goat.

I have known Mr. Tulloch since I was a child. He was an old friend of my father's and Robert Tulloch would often visit us in Kirkwall. He was married then, to a kind, but very quiet woman named Marie. They had two children during that time, but neither lived to see their sixth year. Then Mrs. Tulloch took to bed ill and expired. I was sixteen at the time and already taller than everyone I knew. I would serve tea when Mr. Tulloch, now a widower, would call to visit. Most people found my presence disturbing and would say little to me, but not Robert. He had always been generous with a kind word and would inquire about my happiness. I don't believe courtship was his intention in those days after his wife's passing. He was simply being kind to the peculiar child of an old friend.

The courtship was arranged by my stepmother. I suppose manipulated is a more accurate term. The woman was wily, I'll give her that. The second Mrs. Burness was never warm to me and was eager to jettison the giantess from her home. More than once I overheard her fretting to my father about my marital prospects. What man, she would say, wants a wife who looks down on him? Shortly after the funeral of Marie Tulloch, my stepmother implored the widower to visit often and went out of her way to compliment me to him. How that must have pained her. To this day, I do not know if Robert originally had any plan to court me or if it was all my stepmother's careful machinations. I suppose it doesn't matter. Mr. Tulloch was soon calling at regular intervals, asking to visit with me rather than father. Within two years we were wed, and I was whisked off to the island that Tulloch referred to as a sweet slice of paradise. I was eighteen, he two and thirty.

Enough reminiscences, supper is ready. The children come to the table to find their mother with her hand in the air.

Effie wipes her nose, looking first to me then her father. "Does Mam have a question?"

CHAPTER IV

The Kemp cottage lies directly to the south of our croft, along a footpath of packed earth that snakes through the scrub grass. Mr. Tulloch's catch yesterday was quite plentiful, so I thought I would share some with our closest neighbor. Katie Kemp is a sunny plum of a woman who welcomed me the moment I first set foot on the island. She was the only one, however. The rest still consider me something of an outsider and remain aloof in their dealings with me. I suppose my unmaidenly height does not help in this regard, I don't know.

Katie has six children, all savages, and a lovely man named Tom for a husband. Katie has a big heart, and often goes out of her way to care for others, but it is her own wellbeing that is the reason for my call. She is big in the belly again, and her time is approaching fast.

Their croft is almost identical to ours; a cramped two-room abode that is too small for the number of souls under its roof. My knock is greeted at first by her swelled belly, which protrudes so far that it arrives two minutes before she does.

"Thank God, you're here," Katie says, ushering me in. "Come in, come in, pet."

She waddles back to the table and eases into a chair. The cottage is a bit of a mess and the fire in the hearth almost cold. Five-year-old Simon sits on the floor chewing a piece of dried eel skin.

"What's happened? Are you all right?"

"Pardon the disaster," she says, dismissing the unruly state of her home. "I'm having a rough go at the moment."

"Is it the baby?"

She laughs at this. "It's always the baby. The one on the way or the beasts that are here."

My knuckles touch her brow, fingers probe her throat. I ask about her pain, if there is any discomfort.

"Nothing is comfortable with this one," she assures me. "I'm beyond tired and can't move faster than a snail."

I glance around the cottage but see only young Simon. The boy needs a wash. "Where are the other children?"

"With any luck, they've run away from home." She nods at the open shutter and says they're with their father. "I'd offer tea, but I think my fire's gone out."

"For goodness' sake, Katie. You need to rest up with the babe so close. Hold tight, now."

The ashes in the hearth hold a few glowing embers, but the basket is empty. I bring in more turf from the shed, enough to last a few days and get the fire hot again. Katie tells me of her troubles while I fix a light meal for her. She's grateful but has difficulty eating.

"It burns," she says, wincing at another nibble of saltfish. "No matter what I eat, it scalds my insides."

"Hair," I remark. "The babe already has a full head of it, then."

She covers her mouth to belch. "That'll be a first. All the others were as bald as monks."

I watch her push the plate away. I fear the poor thing is going to bring it all back up, but she grimaces through the discomfort and settles again. We chitchat about her conditions and the trouble that comes with it. She asks about my bandaged thumb and laughs at my clumsiness. Katie adores gossip, so we indulge in it, but it doesn't go very far. With only four families on Eynhallow, there is only so much to wag about. We gab about how my husband and George Heddle like to dip their snout in the drink and how George's wife, Nelly, considers herself so much above everyone here. As a true islander, she has a sharp, judgmental eye, that one. Katie refers to her as the Contessa of Eynhallow, trapped among us serfs. We even take a few swipes at doddering old Hugh Dearness, who reads the Sunday service. He's the closest thing we have to a vicar, but his attempts at sermonizing are both gratingly dull and preposterously rambling. He's a sweet old man, but he should never be allowed near a pulpit.

We even mock each other. She wonders how I'm able to see with my head stuck in the rainclouds and I poke fun at how she manages to stay plump on an island where no one leaves the dinner table satisfied. Were an outsider to overhear us, they might consider us cruel, but the ribbing is good-natured and, I daresay, necessary. Our days are difficult with toil and tedious with drudgery. These little flaying sessions keep us both sane.

Outside of my own children, it is Katie that I hold closest to my heart. She also is not a native islander, which is why we understand one another, but it is her wit and her kindness that keeps me scurrying to her door for companionship. I worry about her. I know she is strong and there are no guarantees, but every woman skates the razor's edge when she brings life into this world. I don't know what I would do if I lost her.

Listen to me. Why does my mind drift to such dark places, I wonder? Katie will be fine. I will make sure nothing bad happens when her time comes.

I insist Katie rest while I tidy up and prepare something that she can throw into the cauldron later for supper. I wet a cloth and wipe Simon's dirty face. The lad bites my finger in response. Poor Katie. She isn't joking when she refers to her brood as little savages.

Mr. Kemp returns home just as I am saying my goodbyes. Tom is a bear of a man, but as gentle as a kitten. He adores Katie, and that is all that matters as far as I am concerned.

My own chores are stacking up at home and I must get on. Katie sees me to the door. She grouses to me about the boredom and how nothing exciting ever happens on this dull island. When I remark that her new babe will be exciting, she just laughs.

"Yes, another miracle of birth," she drolls. "Like that doesn't happen every day. Don't you wish something different would happen? Something to shake us all up?"

"Like what? Do you want to tempt the trolls to crawl out of their caves and eat us?"

"Why not? It'd be better than minding a houseful of brutes."

Walking home through the heather, I am quietly grateful for a friend who can poke a hole through the stuffy veneer of our existence. She reminds me of the jesters of old, the ones who would openly mock the vanity of the royal court.

CHAPTER V

A crab scuttles below the surface of the water, heedless to its doom. I creep up behind it, careful to keep my shadow from scaring it off, and snatch the thing up. My reach is absurdly long, making it easy to poach the little devils from their murky kingdom. I add it to the other three I've caught in the wicker creel. I had a hankering for crab, so I left Grace and Kit to mind the ash pit and came down to the Spur to fish. I catch one more, wading through the cold saltwater, before retreating up the cobble beach. Looking out across the sound, I watch the waves and the mainland shimmer across the sound. The calm of it is soothing, but I must be careful not to drift into a daydream and let the day slip away from me again.

There are times when I remember why I first started gazing out at the sea and there are times when I do not. More of the latter these days. It was a long time ago, a folly of youth and untested hearts. Aren't all of our bad habits formed in our younger days?

This one involved a boy. Sometimes I remember his name and sometimes I do not. James Grieve. Jamie to me, but I was the only one allowed to call him that. We were secret sweethearts back in Kirkwall. Long before Mr. Tulloch and even before the growth spurt that stretched my bones to their painful lengths. Most of my childhood friends shied away after that, but not Jamie. His loyalty remained true because it had already flowered into first love. He was kind and forthright and, to me, beautiful. But he was penniless and fatherless, marking him as the lowest caste in our stuffy community. We were careful to keep our courtship hidden, but secrets are doomed to be outed in any small village. How upset Father was when he found out. My stepmother said nothing, head down as she carried on with her darning, but oh, the smug smirk tipping her pursed lips. Father forbade me from seeing Jamie, threatening to murder the lad if he ever showed his face again. What could I do? I had no authority, no say in the matter. It was shortly after this domestic turmoil that the second Mrs. Burness began her machinations to marry me off to the sad widower, Robert Tulloch. If only I had possessed the brains or the wherewithal to see the clockworks pushing me this way and that. But I did not. I was all of seventeen and heartbroken, cursed to be a spinster as far as I could see. Who wouldn't have fallen for the charms of an older man with prospects and a silver tongue?

Twice Jamie Grieve tried to visit me after my father's banishment and twice his attempts were foiled. The first time he was chased off with a poker from the fire. The second attempt was met with the business end of the family claymore that hung over the mantel. His third attempt succeeded, a week before I was to wed. Jamie scaled the trestle to reach my window and begged me not to go through with my plans. He vowed his love to me, swearing he would raise himself up in the world to earn the right to my hand. He said he would commandeer a boat and sail to Eynhallow to rescue me from a marriage that he knew would not make me happy.

That was the reason I started watching the sea. Why I still watch it to this day, even though I sometimes forget the boy's name. Jamie never appeared, never landed a boat on the shore to honor his vow. His were the hot words of the stupidly enchanted and the recklessly young. I do not begrudge him this. I only hope that he met some other lass and is happy. But this is the root of my habit of staring off at the waves, looking for something that will never appear. A hope or an escape or even a moment's peace. I'll take it, whatever it is.

See how easy it is to slip into reverie and lose track of time? I gather up my shoes and the creel of crabs to make my way home. Climbing from the pebbly beach to the soft clover, I hear an odd calamity of voices in the distance. Cresting the hillock, I spy my husband in the distance, gazing west toward the mainland. Alongside him are his friend, George, and Katie's husband, Tom. And most of our children. The wind carries their voices across the scrub.

"Yonder, there!" exclaims George Heddle. "Tacking our way."

The wind whipsaws his hair about, and he claws it back over his shiny patch. Mr. Heddle is never far from my husband's side. It would be unkind to say he's a bit of a lackey, but if Mr. Tulloch suggested sailing to the moon, George Heddle would be the first one in the boat.

Tom pipes up. "I see it. Who do you suppose it is?"

"Let's hope it's not the laird's man," groans Mr. Tulloch. "With some adjustment to the tenancy."

My children clamor about as I approach, pointing and gesturing at something out to sea.

"What is all the fuss now?"

Effie wants to be picked up. Kit and Meg clamber over each other to be the first one to answer me. Always a competition with these two.

"Look, Mother," shouts Meg. "A boat!"

"A visitor," barks Kit. "Someone important, too."

"Where?"

Grace points. "There."

I follow her direction and, sure enough, there it is. A longboat, making its way across the sound, rowed by two sturdy oarsmen. My childhood foolishness snaps to mind immediately with a single question. Is it Jamie, come at last to take me away? I am such a ninny.

CHAPTER VI

Visitors to our shores are a rare thing, bringing every islander out of their homes to see what the fuss is about. Mr. Tulloch and Mr. Heddle immediately set off to meet the craft landing at the beach. Nelly Heddle and her two boys come down the slope to join Hugh and Mary Dearness. My brood mingles with the Kemp children as Tom and I greet the others. Katie stays indoors as it is unlucky for women in her condition to be seen. The poor thing watches from her door as the assembled crowd gawks at the approaching vessel.

"Who is it?" frets Nelly Heddle, wringing her hands together. She's always been the worrying sort. She nods in greeting but remains as aloof to me as ever.

Mary Dearness is older, about the same age my mother might be had she lived. Mary is fond of saying that gossip is unchristian, but her ears catch every whisper on this isle. I broke our good wash basin a week ago, and Mary knew of it before Mr. Tulloch did. She's all aflutter now, watching the boat land. "What on earth do they want?"

"Oh dear," says her husband, Mr. Hugh Dearness. "It's not the laird, is it?"

I squint, but the beach is too far away to make out any details. "Why would the laird come here?"

"He owns most of the land," says Mr. Dearness.

"Has he ever come before?" I ask.

"No," replies Nelly. Her lips are forever pursed, as if always tasting lemon. "But if it's him, then there's bad news afoot. One of us or all of us."

Conjecture over the arrival of the landowner goes back and forth. Has the laird come to oust someone from their croft and install a new tenant? Clearances happen from time to time, whole families removed from their homes and left destitute. The landowners, with their titles and wealth, can be quite capricious in their appointments. The children run about and get underfoot. My four, plus the two Heddle boys, along with Tom's rampaging children. The mood would almost be festive were it not for the prospect of one family being turned out on their rumps.

Mr. Dearness hurries back to his cottage and returns, wheezing, with a brass spyglass. He clacks the instrument open and puts it to his eye.

"It's not the laird," he reports.

"Then who is it?" asks his wife.

"I don't know," he says. "But the man's come for the long haul, it appears."

Everyone wants to see. I patiently wait my turn with the scope and glass it down to the beach. The two oarsmen are busy unloading a great number of crates and chests onto the pebbly beach. A lone figure directs their movements; a gentleman judging from his fine clothes and dark cloak. Whoever the outlander is, he is no Orkneyman. I am not overly mistrustful, but there is something about his appearance that is off-putting. But now the children are clamoring for a peek so my turn with the glass ends.

Here comes Mr. Tulloch and Mr. Heddle, huffing their way back to us. Both men are immediately assailed with questions. Who is it? What does he want? Is one of us to be evicted?

My husband waves their demands down and catches his breath. George moves on to fetch the horse. Tulloch tells him to bring the nag round our croft, where the wagon is. By now the rest of us are impatient with worry.

"He's a visitor, come for the season," my husband informs us. He enjoys being the focus of attention.

"A visitor?" questions Mr. Dearness. "Here on Eynhallow?"

The question is not a silly one. We do not get travelers or touring guests here. The current on both sides of the island is swift and even deadly to anyone unfamiliar with them.

Nelly's expression sours even more. "Who is he? What does he want?"

"Some foreigner," my husband replies. He holds a letter in his hand, bearing the seal of the laird. "He's leased a cottage from the landowner for the season. That's all I know."

The group of us exchange glances before resuming our questions. Nelly's lips are tighter than a clamshell. "Leased a cottage? Is one of us expected to vacate our home so this foreigner can sleep in a dry bed?"

"Calm down, Nelly," Mr. Tulloch scolds. "No one is being turned out. He's leased the Merryman."

Silence all round. The croft in question is a derelict abode that's stood abandoned for longer than I have lived here. Its stone walls and crumbling roof are now a home for terns and warblers, unfit for human habitation. How on earth is it to be fit for a gentleman of wealth?

"Who would take such a ruin?" asks Mary Dearness. "It's not suitable for a barn."

"To say nothing of the bad spirits," adds her husband. "It is cruel of the laird to lease the man such a foul place."

The Merryman croft lies on the northern rind of the island, near the cliffs. It is said to be haunted, of course.

The clopping of hooves interrupts us as George brings the horse about. Dickie is a handsome bay with a white snout and a gentle demeanor, but he dislikes children. He is well cared for as Dickie is the only horse on the island. He is collectively owned and shared among us, as is the one wagon we possess. Mr. Tulloch and Mr. Heddle lead the horse to the wain, secure it into the harness and walk it down to the beach.

We gawkers go back to conjecturing about the kind of person who would come to live on the island. For a whole season, no less. What could he possibly want? What will he do? None of us have a clue, of course, but that does not stop us from tittering endlessly on things we have no answers to. Such a fuss the man has caused! One thing is abundantly clear—we do not like outsiders here. I know this all too well, but at least I am still Orkney born. Foreigner, Mr. Tulloch had said. How dreadful, gasps Nelly. Some tawdry Continental, adds Mr. Dearness.

To the tiny, enclosed community of Eynhallow, the man may as well be the Devil himself for all the welcome he's about to receive.

CHAPTER VII

We watch the wagon trundle past our door on the rutted track a short time later. Dickie plods along, dipping his head, with George Heddle on the bench and Mr Tulloch on foot, leading the way. The wagon bed is laden with so many crates and portmanteaus that one would think the visitor was settling here for good. Who would bring so many possessions for a summer lease?

Following behind the wagon are the crew of oarsmen. Local boys from Kirkwall. Sturdy lads with strong backs and big hands. I recognize one of them as he sometimes delivers the mail. Bringing up the rear is the stranger himself. I sit outside our cottage peeling potatoes, trying not to be too conspicuous in my curiosity. He is a tall fellow with a straight spine and high chin. His brow is lofty, his hair dark. Handsome in an angular fashion, but there is a dark intensity to his gaze and an impatience in his step. Nobility perhaps, or just haughtiness, I cannot say. I don't know if I have ever been the best judge of character, to be fair. He is of means which is apparent from the fine cut of his clothes. An abrupt wind knocks the hat from his head and sends it rollicking across the heath. He seems amused by this but makes no move to chase after it. Kit and Meg are both halfway across the island, chasing it down.

Curiously, the stranger stops every so often to look behind him and scan the lay of the land. Is he looking for someone in particular or is he troubled by the tingling sensation of being followed? So much mystery! The stranger and the reasons for his visit will dominate the chitchat among us for weeks to come.

"He looks odd," remarks Grace. She shares the bench and the labor with me.

"Don't stare, dear. Odd how?"

The girl shrugs. "I'm not sure if I can put my finger on it. Different, I suppose. But mean-spirited, too."

I steal another glance at the visitor. "Mean? How do you deduce that?"

"Look at him scowl," she says. "He looks like he's got a mouthful of spoiled oyster."

30

I admonish her for being quick to judge, but I laugh all the same. Within a few minutes, the wagon and party crests the hill and sinks from sight.

Grace takes the potatoes inside while I gather the peels and call for Daisy. Outside of a dog, I have never known an animal to respond to its own name, yet Daisy comes running every time. She brays happily and loudly as she laps up the potato rinds, which muffles the approach of another visitor this day.

Katie is always keen on a good jest and never passes up an opportunity to goose me, which she does now. I startle, squeal, and laugh, in that order.

"Katherine Jane, what are you doing out here? You should be at home."

She blows a curl out of her eye. "I'm tired of being cooped up. I wanted to see what all the fuss was about."

"Sit," I insist, leading her to the bench. "You can't be out frolicking in your state. You'll only attract nasty attention."

Katie scoffs. "Don't start with that nonsense."

"Make some room, you cow." Squeezing next to her on the bench, I scan the terrain south to be sure none of our neighbors can see Katie flouting convention. "It doesn't matter what I believe. Nelly believes it and she'll cause a bloody row if she sees you outdoors."

"That stupid woman and her rules. Bah."

It is dangerous for an expectant mother to be out in public. It is considered shameful, of course, but it also risks attracting the unwanted attention of the trolls and faery folk. They love nothing more than to pester pregnant mothers or to snatch their babes from their cribs. It may sound absurdly backwards, which of course it is, but the islanders believe it nonetheless. The Heddles and the Dearness clans hold themselves higher in station to Katie and I, and the last thing we need is to give them something new to tut about.

With one hand draping her belly, Katie turns to me with bright eyes. "So? Who is this strange man? Did you get a good look at him?"

"Not really. He seems the stuffy sort, to be honest."

My friend's curiosity runs as deep as my own, but I have little in the way of information. She is as astonished as I to learn that the stranger has leased the old Merryman croft.

"Why the devil would he lease that ruin? It's nothing but cobwebs and tern nests. God, the bird lime alone in that place."

Again, I have nothing to satisfy her. Not that it matters, of course. Katie is perfectly happy to improvise a whole bushel of reasons for this visit, each one more fantastical than the one before.

"Maybe he's running from something. A baron, cast out of his native land and forced into exile. Or maybe he's one of those mad poets you hear about. He's come to run naked along the heath and scream his rhymes to the heavens."

"My God, can you imagine the scandal?"

"I'd welcome it," she says. "I can think of worse things than a naked gent on the heath." My elbow goes sharp into her ribs. "You're incorrigible."

She flashes a mischievous smile. "Just uncomfortable. I get flushed all the time now, and the only thing that brings relief is a good rollicking."

"Shush now." I glance about for prying ears. Fortunately, the children are nowhere to be seen.

I enjoy Katie's imagination. It always tacks to the extreme. Mine is a bit pedestrian in comparison. My friend likes to scandalize me with all her bawdy talk. "Maybe the laird swindled the poor man, selling him the idea that Eynhallow was a beautiful holiday location?"

She laughs. "I wouldn't put it past him, the greedy goat. Oh! What if the stranger is a fugitive? A fiend running from the law of his country after slicing a few pretty throats!"

"Katie, no. I'll have nightmares now."

At this, Katie pushes me off the bench. "What do you have to be afraid of? You could crush his skull in one of those powerful mitts of yours!"

From anyone else, this remark would be cutting. Katie and I know each other well enough to trade prickly barbs about our shortcomings. A sport that passes the time. I pat her knee.

"Come on, then. Let's get your wide bottom home. Can you manage or should I fetch the wheelbarrow?"

"Ooh, you're a ripe sow, you know that?" She flounders to get up and then laughs when I pull her to her feet. My waddling friend is slow, and it takes a good while to escort her safely home. Thankfully, there is no one downslope to spy on us.

Katie thanks me for the guard duty, but her demeanor shifts, and the levity blows away on the wind.

"Lord only knows who the man is and why he's here. Your cottage is closest to Merryman's. Maybe lock your door tonight."

Her advice is preposterous. "What a thing to say. Go put those feet up."

I promise to check on her tomorrow and admonish the children to look after their mother. Willmouse, Katie's oldest boy, promises to do his best, while his brother, Simon, dangles like an ape from a ceiling beam.

On the footpath home, I am bemused by Katie's suggestion of a locked door. No one locks their doors on this island. A barred door is an affront to the spirits who come out after dark. They would kick it in and tear our cottage apart at such an insult. Still, her bloodthirsty imagination has my nerves a little raw when I return home. Inside, I find my usual catastrophe of a family. Grace sits before the hearth with a book in her lap, tutoring Kit his letters. Effie is squealing in delight because her sister, Meg, has tied a bonnet over Daisy's horns.

"Look, Mam," Effie sings. "Meg has made Daisy pretty!"

Saints in a rowboat, how has it come to this?

CHAPTER VIII

When Mr. Tulloch returns from delivering the visitor to his leased cottage, I ambush him with questions about the stranger. Frustratingly, Mr. Tulloch has little to illuminate any of the mystery. My husband is prone to become cross when waylaid with too many questions. His patience only goes so far, you see.

"He's rich and he's rude," he says. "What else is there to know?"

"Why is he here? Did he not say anything?"

The cork on the jug is popped. "Not a word. He was in a hurry to shoo us out of there, I can tell you that."

I swear the man goes out of his way just to grind my nerves. "An impatient man, then?" I remark. "Well, what else, Robert? Don't be stingy now."

"He's a foreigner. But he didn't say where from. The man spoke French and something else. German, maybe."

It's like pulling teeth with this man. "All right. And does this foreigner have a name?"

"Aye. A funny sounding one, too. But I don't remember it now. Firkin-von-lederhosen or some such thing."

"For heaven's sakes, Robert. You can't remember the man's name?"

He tilts his snout into the cauldron over the fire, testing its aroma. "Ah, Agnes. What does it matter? Stop now."

"You're impossible. A complete stranger shows up out of the blue to stay for the season and you don't want to know why?"

Mr. Tulloch lifts the spoon to taste what I've cooked. He is not thrilled. "Is this really what we're supping on?"

"You can go without, if you like."

Mr. Tulloch drops into a chair with a long sigh. "I don't know what you want to hear, Agnes. He's a pompous gent with rude manners and little regard for people below his station. And he was eager to get us out of his hair."

"What do you mean?"

"You know how bad that house is. No one's lived there in thirty years. I apologized for the state of the place, explaining that I had no warning of his coming. Otherwise, I would have had the place made habitable. He didn't care. When I offered to get the fire going, he told me not to bother. He just wanted me and the oarsmen gone." Mr. Tulloch digs into a vest pocket and claps a coin on the table. "He was generous, though. I'll give him that."

The coin is shiny, and it rings smartly on the wood. A day's wages in these parts, and then some. Mr. Tulloch sweeps it from the table, and drops it back into his pocket, looking very pleased with himself.

Dram money, I'm sure of it. I have little hope that this unexpected boon will go towards any of our outstanding debts to the laird or food for the table. Fresh thatch for the crumbling roof. I can't help wonder if he does this just to flounce me. I have no say when it comes to shillings and crowns. Married though I am, I may as well be a pauper for all the say I have in the distribution of capital in this family.

Vexing indeed.

Sunday arrives, and along with it, the unpleasant struggle to make the children presentable for church. Meg refuses to wear her good dress and Kit won't stop tugging at his collar. Effie is not feeling well and wants to be carried as we march through the tussock grass to the ruins on the southern bow of the island. With no vicar here, Mr. Hugh Dearness performs scriptural readings on Sunday in lieu of a proper service. During winter, this takes place in the Dearness cottage. It is one of the larger crofts on the island, but it is still a cramped place when twenty parishioners squeeze into it. Summers are more pleasant as Mr. Dearness does the reading at the kirk ruins not far from where he and Mrs. Dearness reside.

The walls and archways of the ruins are made of slabs of sandstone and will probably stand for all eternity, but the roof collapsed long ago. The ruins are the largest and most elaborate structure on the island, but their origin remains a mystery as no one really knows who built them. Eynhallow is awash in mystery, and the legends often contradict one another. Was the island christened the "holy isle" because of the kirk or was it built because the island is holy?

One thing is certain; the place feels sacred. The urge to lower one's voice and bow the head feels instinctual among these ancient stone walls. Mr. Dearness reads from Paul's letters to the Corinthians and the Ephesians, which he follows up with something like a sermon, but it rambles and makes little sense. Still, we all nod along and pretend that the dunderheaded homily sounds like wisdom.

The true appeal of church is the chance to socialize when service is concluded. The children are finally unchained and let loose to rampage through the stone walls while the adults commune over shared hardship. Under normal circumstances, the conversation tips to talk of the weather, the fishing, or the price of flour. But not today. All anyone wants to discuss is the stranger in our midst and his mysterious reasons for coming to Eynhallow. The stranger's absence at Sunday service is marked by all, which leads to the question of the man's moral and religious character. Is he a heathen or, even worse, one of these radical atheists one hears about?

Mr. Dearness, who is kind and gentle above all things, is surprisingly harsh in his judgment of the fellow in the derelict cottage. The man, he declares, is an apostate of the worst sort. Yesterday, Mr. Dearness made the long walk up to the Merryman croft to invite the newcomer to services only to be met with cool indifference. The foreigner claimed to be too busy to attend church. That left poor Mr. Dearness apoplectic.

"Too busy?" he sputters. "Imagine being too busy to redeem one's soul? Too busy for the Almighty? The very idea."

Mrs. Dearness fans her face as if she's about to swoon. "Disgraceful," she adds.

"I'm glad he didn't come," says Nelly Heddle. "We don't want that sort sullying our worship."

A public flaying is in the air, so I slip out of the conversation before blood is spilt. The foreign gent and his audacious absence from Sunday worship is like cream to hungry cats. The islanders will dine on this subject for days to come. I have no desire to participate in the bloodbath, having been on the receiving end of it in the past. What confounds me is this need to cut someone to ribbons for their faults and sins, believing the contrast will highlight the cutter's own superior nature. Making oneself taller by standing on another is an ugly play in my opinion.

I wish Katie were here. Sundays are always better when she's not hidden away like some shameful thing. It seems so silly and unnecessary. Everyone on the island knows she is with child and yet she must stay indoors for fear of offending anyone with her swelled belly? How outcast and alone she must feel right now, excluded from something whose very purpose is to bring people together.

CHAPTER IX

Two days pass without any sighting of the mysterious visitor. At least during the day. George Heddle claims he saw the stranger late at night, walking the beach. Our neighbor said the man was talking to himself in his foreign tongue, leading George to wonder if the man is mad. Mind you, it was after midnight and Mr. Heddle would have been well into his cups by then so I cannot say how reliable his report is. No one has seen the stranger leave his cottage, which leads Mr. Tulloch to speculate if the man's hung himself from a ceiling timber.

"Another ghost for an already haunted croft," he laughs.

I tell him not to frighten the children. He tells me not to be such a humorless clam.

"Everyone loves a ghost story," he adds, before leaving the table.

There are times when Mr Tulloch and I get along fine, but there are long stretches when we simply tolerate one another. Lately, however, the air between us has become chilly. I have no idea why, but patience seems to be running thin for both of us. Katie also mentions to me that she is feeling a little tension between herself and Tom. Much of it has to do with the strain of her condition, but there is something else at play, she feels. She wonders if it is the stranger among us. The man has brought a cloud of ill temper with him, pestering the entire isle with it. I laugh at this notion, but she remarks that we have not had a lick of sunshine since the man arrived. Is it coincidence, these overcast days, or something more? I tell her she is simply bored from being cooped up too long and her brains are running hot.

Later this day, the stranger appears. Grace and I are weeding the garden rows when Meg pipes up behind us.

"Mother, look," she says. "That man is here."

On the far side of the property, where the low stone fence meets the footpath, is the mysterious guest to our shores. He does not appear to be faring well. His hair is unkempt and blowing in the wind, and his clothes look limp and disheveled. He stands speaking with Mr. Tulloch. They are downwind from us, so their conversation is whisked off in the wrong direction for me to catch. I watch my husband listen and nod his head. The stranger dips into a vest pocket and places something in my husband's palm. They shake hands and then the man turns and marches back uphill to his cottage. Mr. Tulloch, the oaf, simply picks up his rake and goes back to work. Some days I just want to box the man's ears.

I march over to him. "What was all that about?"

"Our guest is having a spot of domestic calamity, it seems," Mr. Tulloch says. "The ass."

"What does that mean? What did he give you? Was it money?"

The object is still in his hand. Two shillings. "The man is in need of a wife," he laughs.

My patience thins. "Is that a joke?"

"He needs someone to cook and clean for him," he says, pocketing the coins.

The grin on his face is profoundly smug. "Robert," I warn him. "Tell me you didn't."

My husband just keeps grinning. "Now, now, Agnes. The man's paying handsomely. Who am I to say no?"

"If you think I am going to cook and clean for that man, you are out of your bleeding mind. I have more than I can handle as it is around here."

He takes up the rake again. "It's a golden opportunity," he says. "And believe me, we need the money, Agnes."

"Then you go be his washerwoman," I spit back at him. "I'll have nothing to do with it."

My husband talks to my back as I walk away. "Winter's coming, my dear. And the catch is getting stingier every time I go out. You know this. Our children are going to have to grit down and go hungry till the spring comes."

He's not wrong, damn him. The fishing has been terrible this season and we will feel it come Christmastime. We lost two of our goats in a bad storm this April, leaving only Daisy. No milk to sell to the neighbors. Shillings from a foreigner will keep the winter wolves from our door.

I stop and turn. "I will bring the man his supper. Nothing fancy, just a pot of whatever we are eating. And I'll sweep the cottage. No more."

He tips his hat to me. "There's a good girl."

"Don't say that." I stride back into the house before I say something I will regret. How easy it is for my husband to give away time I do not have to spare.

Banging at the door rattles me awake. It is dark and the candle is long snuffed out. A visitor at this hour can only mean disaster or death. The person outside our door is calling my name. I hurry to unlatch it, finding young Will. Katie's oldest boy. He is out of breath and agitated.

"What is it, Willmouse? Is your mother all right?"

"My father sent me," the boy pants. "He says it's time."

The babe. I snatch the cloak from the peg and wake my eldest. If the babe is really on its way, then I'll need Grace's help and it's time she learned the way of it.

"Grace, get dressed and meet me at the Kemp croft. Quickly now."

I hurry out the door and follow young Will, not even bothering with shoes. I expect to find the Kemp cottage in chaos, but this proves not to be the case. Katie is on her feet, warming herself before the fire. Tom is pacing the floor with an ashen face.

It is a false alarm. Katie had some pain and a few spasms, but the baby is not on its way this night. Tom apologizes for waking me, but I tell him there's no need. One cannot be too careful at the last stages. When Grace arrives breathless at the door, Tom begs her forgiveness also. I send Grace back home and get Katie settled.

"Are you sure you're all right?" I ask her. "The discomfort is gone?"

"It's passed, whatever it was." Katie drums her fingers along her belly. "The little pest loves nothing more than to trouble me."

I probe her belly with my fingers. It is hard, the skin stretched firm, but I feel nothing irregular. "Anything out of the usual?"

"Oh, I don't know. What's usual when it comes to this?"

With the emergency over, I say goodnight and take the pathway home. A cloudless night lights my way through the knapweed and bluebells. It never gets truly dark here in the summer months. The land is a black silhouette against the twilit sea. I stop halfway to listen to the eternal lap of the surf on the shore and drink in the cool vastness of the twinkling waves before me. It is the kind of blissful peace that, if you listen closely, you can hear the breath of God moving on the face of the waters.

But I am not alone in my nocturnal worship. Down the slope to the waterline is a figure moving over the craggy rocks of the shore. Difficult to see, as the figure is naught but a shape of solid black against the dark sea. My first assumption is that it is our mysterious visitor, traipsing about after midnight, but that cannot be. The figure is enormous and malformed. Taller even than myself and I am the tallest individual on the island. Immediately, my mind turns to the specters of legend that are said to haunt Eynhallow. The trolls from the caves or the Nordic spirits who shriek through the night, eager to tear apart any fool out in the open. Like me.

Eynhallow

My pace doubles and I keep my eyes on the spectral shadow, praying it does not hear me. My prayers are wasted as I see the inky giant turn and amble my way with great strides. My own strides are nothing to sneeze at as I break into a mad sprint for home. I almost take the front door clean off clamoring to get inside. I slam it shut and shoulder it home, anticipating the blow of the dark figure barreling into it. I catch my breath, but no impact touches the door. My hands are trembling from the excitement, and I do not think I will be able to sleep this night. I listen to the snores and sighs of my sleeping family. No one was awakened by my calamitous, and very noisy, return. The sleep of the innocent, I suppose.

Pouring some water from the pitcher, I sit and wait for my nerves to calm, my mind reeling with one thought: who, or what, is out there skulking through the night?

CHAPTER X

Mr. Tulloch is unconcerned when I relay the details of my nighttime fright. A trick of the eyes, he says, distorted by sea and moonlight. I make no mention of ogres or the ghosts of old Norsemen. I pare my description down to a very tall and oddly shaped figure loping over the rocks like an animal.

"It must have been the foreign gent," he says. "Out for a midnight jaunt. The lunatic."

"But it was massive," I counter. "I've never seen anything so tall."

He brushes it away like crumbs from the table. "Darkness plays tricks, Agnes. If it was that tall, maybe you saw your own reflection in the water."

Very droll, that is. I can see he will not allow any relevance to what I saw last night. Still, I try. "Is it possible someone else is on the island? That someone slipped ashore under the cover of night?"

To his credit, he weighs this possibility before answering. "You know how rough that current gets. Choppy as pandemonium under the best of conditions. Any fool attempting a landing in the dark would have gone under or been whisked out to sea."

Irked, I bang the pot and turn to the window. His hand touches my shoulder, his voice tempering to a gentler tone.

"I've no doubt you saw something," he says. "But I doubt it was a giant, as you say. The moon is a fickle lady. She loves to play her tricks on us."

I sigh and tell him he's probably right. I'm already doubting the whole experience. Maybe I dreamt the whole thing.

"Don't forget," he adds, "You're to bring our guest his dinner and see about the condition of the place. There's a good girl."

That phrase again. I don't know why my husband employs this two-handed cuff where a moment's gentleness is followed by a tweak of the nose. First the sugar, then the vinegar. Never just the sweetness. It's how he treats the children, too.

Late into the day, I tell the children to listen to their older sister while I head out across the heath to the north end with a small pot of stew and a heel of bread wrapped in cloth. I am more than a little vexed at these additional chores placed at my feet. The foreigner is clearly a man of wealth. Surely, he could have brought along a footman or a cook to see to his comfort? What was he thinking, coming here alone?

The prospect of entering that decrepit bulding also has my nerves on edge. Merryman cottage is a forlorn and ugly ruin, and there is no lack of ghostly tales about the grim place. It was built decades ago by a retired sea captain named Merryman for his new bride, a young lass from Aberdeen. She was a city girl from a good family, and half the age of her groom. She did not fare well on this windswept, lonely isle. She claimed to hear ghosts rattling the cupboards and see spirits dancing on the shore. She complained of the wind that never stops, saying she heard voices whispering in it. That part I can empathize with. The same infernal wind rattled my own sanity in my first year on Eynhallow.

Captain Merryman dismissed his bride's claims and, being a hardened seaman, quieted her with a firm hand. She died of a broken skull, the result of a kick from a horse, as the sea captain explained. The young bride was buried on the property under a monument of marble slab shipped from Carrara. Alone in the sad cottage he had built, Captain Merryman began to unravel. He told his neighbors that he heard his wife's voice whisper to him on the wind, that he saw her shadow at the foot of his bed. He became a recluse after this, rarely leaving the croft. Concerned, his neighbors went to check on him and found the sea captain lifeless in his bed. Cradled in his arms were the bones of his dead wife. A ghastly scene, to be sure. Out in the yard lay a massive hole under the marble headstone. Had the man gone mad and exhumed his dead wife or did the bride claw her way out of the grave to plant the kiss of death on her husband? The former sounded more reasonable than the latter, but no one really knew what went on inside those walls. With the windows shuttered and the door sealed, the place was declared uninhabitable and remained abandoned. Until now, that is.

I am not a keen observer of ghost tales or stories of haunted abodes. They pass the time on dreary winter nights, I suppose. And yet, I cannot help wondering what kind of person could live in the squalid confines of Merryman croft. I have half a mind to leave the man's supper outside the front door and run home.

No one answers my knock or responds to my hallos. The door lags and needs a push to open. The interior is dark, and it smells of mildew. Cobwebs drape from every angle and a muddy bird's nest sits atop the broad mantel. There are wooden crates stacked everywhere and odd-looking equipment on the floor and piled atop the long table. Straw packing is littered everywhere, and the hearth is cold. On the far side of the room is a measly cot pushed up against the wall.

How on earth can someone live in this mess?

When it was built, Merryman was the finest cottage on the island. There is a main hall with two closed doors at the back and a loft above. I announce myself loudly, shouting another hallo, to an obviously empty home. Where is the tenant? No matter. I get the fire started and hook the pot on the transom bar to warm the fellow's supper. The two oil lamps are lit but they do little to dispel the gloom of the place. It takes a moment to find the broom among all the crates and I spend a good deal of time sweeping all the damn straw out the door. It is almost ankle deep.

The doors to both inner rooms are closed. The first opens to a completely barren space save for a pile of books in the corner. I snoop through each book but not one volume is written in English. How vexing. I could murder someone for a new book to read. The east wall is covered in strange markings and ciphers, I don't know. Someone has taken chalk and scribbled all kinds of nonsense on the smooth surface of the horsehair cement. Did the new tenant scribe this or were these marks always here? The other door is locked and will not open.

I go back to my tidying, removing first the desiccated nest on the mantel. The thing is old and nigh cemented to the beam with a few broken eggshells in the bowl. It has served its purpose, sheltering the chicks until they flew the coop and bred chicks of their own. I wonder if the birdlings were troubled by the ghosts of the old sea captain and his dead bride.

Pulling a stool up before the hearth, I stir the pot to see if it's warmed yet. A voice startles me from behind. I turn to see a man with a pistol aimed at my heart.

"Who are you?" he demands.

"Mrs. Tulloch. You spoke to my husband yesterday."

His expression wrinkles. "The cook?"

"I agreed to bring you supper," I say, indicating the pot warming in the hearth. "But I am not your cook. Could I trouble you to point that nasty thing elsewhere?"

He looks at the flintlock in his hand like he's surprised to find it there. He lowers the barrel to the floor and disengages the strike hammer. "I am so sorry. Forgive me."

Common advice tells us not to judge one's appearance, but, in truth, I do it all the time. Especially now, with so much mystery clouding the stranger. His looks are fair, and his hair even has a few curls about it, so prized among his class. The eyes are broodingly dark, the brow tall, a strong nose. I will say he is not unhandsome, and leave it at that. Aristocratic and noble born, that much is apparent, but there is something oddly ragged about the man. It might be the rumple to his fine clothes or the way his eyes dart about in a frenzy. He seems tormented and jittery, not unlike a fugitive on the run. Maybe Katie is correct after all. How delighted she'll be to learn that.

"You were expecting an enemy?" I ask, nodding at the pistol.

"What? No." Flustered by the pistol in his hand, he upends the weapon, knocks the powder into a saucer and sets the flintlock on the mantel. The gunblack leaves his hand sooty.

"I am sorry," he says. Then he looks at the floor, puzzled. "You cleaned?"

"I swept the floor." I wave the spoon at the strange equipment piled on the floor and stacked on the table. "I didn't know what to do with those odd things. What is it?"

"Instruments," he says. "Please, do not touch any of it."

"I don't intend to. Sir, I don't know what Mr. Tulloch told you, but I do not have time to be your washerwoman. I will bring you supper and sweep, but no more."

The new tenant busies himself with his "instruments" on the table, paying me little heed. "Yes, yes, that is fine."

Grateful sort, isn't he? I'll admit I've never met any highborns, but his rudeness is no surprise. These noble types truly think they are above the rest of us. I test the stew again. Warm enough.

"There now, your dinner is ready." I rise from the stool and bring the pot to the table. "Do you possess a bowl among your instruments? Or a spoon?"

The man looks up from his strange tools, and his eyes widen in an awful manner. One that I know all too well, unfortunately. I tower over the foreigner by a full head.

"My word," he gasps with upturned eyes. "Your height…"

He is neither the first rude man I have met, nor will he be the last. "Yes, I am aware, thank you." Among the clatter of vials and tubes on the table, I spy a spoon. A measuring spoon, to be precise. I assume it to be pewter but am surprised to find it is sterling silver. I hand it to him. "Here. Eat before it gets cold."

It takes a moment for him to drag his gaze from me to the steaming pot before him. His demeanor shifts forthwith as he snatches the spoon and digs into the stew, eating it straight from the pot.

"Thank you," he says with a full mouth. He ravages the meal like a Hun. "I haven't eaten in days."

The gratitude is appreciated. I make for the door. "I'll be on my way then, sir."

"I'm sorry, Frau. What did you say your name was?"

"I am Mrs. Tulloch. Agnes, if you prefer."

He rises, wipes his mouth, and extends a hand. "Thank you again, Frau Tulloch. Your stew is delicious."

"That's very kind of you, sir."

I'm anticipating a handshake, but the man rotates my hand and plants a kiss upon my knuckles like a suitor at a ball. This gesture may be a regular part of his high-minded world, but it startles me.

"You have saved a wretched life, Frau Tulloch. Danke."

He still hasn't released my hand. Heat flushes my cheeks and I withdraw my hand, resetting the decorum. "That seems a little dramatic, but it is appreciated, Mr…?"

"Frankenstein," he says. "Victor Frankenstein."

"Very good. I will be back tomorrow then, Mr…er, sir." There is no way I can reiterate that surname, so I don't even try. Closing the door behind me, I hurry down the path to our cottage in the distance. For once, Mr. Tulloch is right. The new tenant does have a ridiculous sounding name.

CHAPTER XI

A routine clicks into place. My days are spent caring for the children and the never-ending chores of the home. By late afternoon I prepare the meal, stealing a spoonful here and there as I won't be dining with my family. I put Grace in charge of supper and carry a pot up the path to the lonely croft to feed the tenant and tidy up as best as I can. What on earth is the man up to? Every evening I arrive to find some new catastrophe of broken glass or a sooty black mark on the wall as if from some burst of flame. One night it is a frothing mixture that seems to eat away at the wood of the table, the next night there is a pool of blood on the floor. Where the blood came from is beyond me. Mr. Franken-something-something seems unharmed and there is no one else here. Maybe he snatched a tern or puffin from the rocky cliffs.

He is a strange creature, this foreigner with the funny name. Most evenings, he ignores me as he is consumed in his strange work. He talks to himself and sometimes curses. Sometimes in French, and other times in German. On occasion he hurls a glass beaker against the wall in frustration. The cot in the corner is rarely used as the man seems to work night and day. It is taking its toll as he is quite haggard looking, and I admonish him to get some rest. He brushes this aside, telling me he will sleep when he's dead. Arriving at the cottage last night, I found the man head down on the table in a profound sleep. I was unsure of what to do but letting him doze among the cruel-looking instruments and flutes of diabolical liquids seemed dangerous. I eased the man into my arms and laid him out on the cot. Not a difficult task, as I have mentioned my unusual strength, which is advantageous to me in circumstances like these.

The tenant seems bewildered and a little cowed when I arrive at the croft tonight. I hang the pot in the hearth and rekindle the neglected fire. There is a fresh stain splattered all over the east wall. Greenish in color, with a faint smell of rotting citrus to it.

"I see the work continues apace," I say, looking over the green stain. "Dare I ask what happened here?"

"A failure," he says quietly. "One of many."

The stain is revolting. It seems to have eaten away at the very stone. "I am not touching this poison."

"Yes, of course," he says distractedly. He looks at me, brow furrowed. "Mrs. Tulloch, did you put me to bed last night?"

"Agnes, please. And yes, I did. You were unconscious at the table, among all those things of yours."

His face reddens. "You didn't have to do that. That must have been a struggle."

"It was no bother at all, Mr. Franken…" I stop, compose myself. "May I call you Victor? I apologize, but I cannot help but giggle when I say your name."

This takes him by surprise. "It is a very proud name, I'll have you know. The Frankensteins go back a long way, masters of—"

My laughter is abrupt and rude, interrupting him. I curtsy and apologize.

"I suppose it is a mouthful on the English tongue. Please, call me Victor."

The broom is in the corner. I put it to use sweeping more straw out the door. Where does it all come from? Turning, I see him scrutinizing me in a way that makes me blush.

"You are a curious study, Agnes," he says. Arms folded, one finger tapping his lips. "Your height is extraordinary. And you say you ferried me from the table all the way to the cot with no trouble?"

"Yes, sir. I am no fainting milkmaid."

"Indeed." His eyes narrow, his scrutiny deepens to the point it almost cuts. "May I measure you?"

"I beg your pardon?"

"Your height," he says. Rooting through the mess of books and tools on the table, he produces a tailor's tape. "Your girth, your breadth. Your skull, also."

What a preposterous thing to request? To say nothing of its rudeness. Yet he seems oblivious to this, clearly expecting me to comply. Is this how the ruling class address their inferiors? Rude demands and no manners?

"That would be unpleasant, sir," I respond. "Thank you, no."

The man is taken aback, but then shakes his head as if coming to his senses. "Yes, of course. I must sound like an ass to you. It is part of my work, you see. Nothing untoward or diabolical, I assure you."

"I see." My eyes roll over the crates and the odd-looking tools on the table. There are books and papers scattered about, alongside surgical knives and coils of strange tubing. "What exactly is your work, if I may ask."

He frowns and scratches his chin as if struggling to answer. "It is scientific. The natural philosophies. Chemistry, galvanism, dynamism. Right now, my focus is on anatomy. In all its glorious variance. That is the purpose behind my request."

It all sounds like gibberish when it's strung together like corn on a string. But I am not completely unschooled. "Anatomy? That is the study of the body, yes?"

"It is," he says with surprise. "Are you educated?"

"No, sir. But I have read about the medical college in Edinburgh. It is well regarded when it comes to anatomy. And all the unseemly news about their use of cadavers."

He strikes a match to light the lamp. "Yes, that is a bit of a scandal. I was just there, you know. Consulting with the professors, before coming here."

There is something unnerving in that remark. "I see. Are you one of these dissectionists everyone is all up in arms about?"

"It is one area of my studies, but not the focus. I notch my arrow on something far loftier."

The man enjoys a riddle, I see. "And what would that be, sir?"

The eyes. Something glassy and far away glistens in them. "A spark of the divine."

He jests, thinking me the fool. "Well, best of luck with that, Victor. I should be on my way."

"So soon?" He seems genuinely disappointed. "I'm rather enjoying your company. It's ironic, really. I came here for the solitude, but I was not prepared for how lonely it would truly be. I enjoy your visits. They keep me sane."

I finish wiping down the table and hang the cloth on a peg. "You need a wife, sir. A companion and confidant."

"Yes, I suppose I do." He scratches his chin again, mulling something over. "Oddly enough, that too is part of my work."

"That makes no sense, sir. Are you jesting again?"

"No. Forgive me, I become distracted at times." He crosses the room to stand before me. His head tilts up to meet me. "Agnes, would you do me this great favor and let me take your measure? It would aid me so much in my studies. You are one of the most remarkable souls I have ever met."

I have no wish to be measured like a side of beef, but I have difficulty saying no. Politeness overrules my qualms, and his tone grinds away my reservation. "Very well," I sigh. "But be quick about it and please, please, mind your etiquette."

"Of course, of course," he says, happily spooling out his tape.

48

Here I stand, feeling like a tailor's dummy while he stretches his tape up and down and across. Taking a sheaf of paper, he sketches out my frame and adds the measurements to the sketch. It is awkward and I cannot stop my cheeks from reddening. I am not acquainted with attention like this, but it is not as unpleasant as I had anticipated.

"Thank you, my friend," he says, tossing the tape onto the table. "Aside from making me happy, you have aided the progress of science this night!"

He seems giddy and almost drunk with joy. My employer sees me to the door, shakes my hand briskly, and releases me into the night. It is only after a few paces that I realize he has slipped a coin into my hand. A green shilling, no less.

CHAPTER XII

I am thrilled with the extra wages, but I kick myself for mentioning it to Mr. Tulloch. He takes it from my palm, reminding me that it is the husband's duty to be steward of the family purse. When I protest, he cites Paul's letter to the Ephesians, adding that women do not possess heads for figures and will not hear otherwise. The shilling goes into his pocket and there is no more to say on the matter.

My frustrations are put to one side as Effie is doing poorly again. She is listless and her brow is hot with fever. Will this poor thing never know a day of good health? When her eyes roll lazily in their sockets, I become alarmed. I direct Grace to cool her brow with a cold cloth while I mix a compress to plaster on the child's chest. It has worked in the past and I pray it will work again. My youngest complains of the smell, but I tell her not to touch it. She sleeps now, thank the Lord.

The sun sets on another day and I hurry with the meal, reserving a little in a bowl, and run it up to the lonely cottage on the cliff. Our visitor is happy to see me. He tells me has worked around the clock but is tired of his own company and welcomes my visit.

"I cannot stay," I tell him. "I'm sorry."

"Why not? I have been talking to myself all day and fear I'm losing my mind." He does look a little sallow, with green hollows under those intense eyes.

"My daughter is not well," I say, setting the bowl on the table. "My youngest, Effie. She's prone to the fevers. I can't leave her."

"I see. Of course." His disappointment is genuine. The man seems lonely.

"If the fever breaks, I will be back tomorrow evening."

He rubs his jaw in thought, and then asks about Effie. How old she is, how much she weighs. About other complaints such as vomiting or dysentery. Tooth loss, of all things. He listens carefully, weighing each reply, then he opens a portmanteau and roots through its many compartments. He folds an envelope out of a sheet paper and dispenses a measure of white powder into it and places it in my hand.

"Here," he says. "This might help the child."

"What is it?"

"A restorative powder. It's known to break fevers and bring rest. Give her just a little at a time. A fourth of a teaspoon, dissolved in water, and mind her reaction."

I am taken aback at the generosity. "Thank you. That is very kind."

"Goodnight, Agnes. And Godspeed."

The next day is spent at my child's bedside. Euphemia's fever deepens and my worst fears bubble up. I neglect everything but her, and Mr. Tulloch complains, but I will not lose another child. When his grousing gets too loud, I threaten to stab him in his sleep, and he barges out of the cottage. I administer the powder Victor provided, but it doesn't break the fever. Effie's eyes roll over white and she mewls like an abandoned kitten. It is torture, and it carries on all night and into the next day.

Grace, bless her heart, takes care of her siblings for me. She feeds them and keeps them out of trouble, tells them not to worry about their baby sister. When I ask her to run a meal up to the guest at Merryman croft, she refuses. She does not like the looks of the stranger and refuses to go anywhere near that haunted place. I don't scold her. The new tenant will simply have to fend for himself.

I administer more of the powder and by dawn of the next day, it seems to have had an effect. Effie's fever breaks and her eyeballs right themselves in their little sockets. She stops sounding like a dying kitten and says she's frightfully hungry. I dampen her precious face with my tears and thank God for his divine mercy. He has taken enough of my babes as it is and spares this little one.

"There, there," Effie coos as she wraps her small arms around my neck. "Now you rest, and I will take care of you."

The tears run anew. All my children have moments of sweetness, but Effie never fails to hoist my heart into my throat.

With lifted spirits, I get busy with the chores that I've neglected. The day is bright, and Effie wants to sit outside. She's not recovered enough to play with her siblings, but she sits contentedly feeding cowslip petals to the goat while Meg climbs the cottage to steal eggs from the tern's nest on the roof. Mr. Tulloch returns home with the herring he netted earlier. I cook it up and get the family situated at the dinner table to eat. A good portion of fish is wrapped up and I hurry along to feed the lonely tenant uphill. With Grace refusing to bring food, the man must be starving.

The cottage is a disaster. More strange substances have stained the walls and the place reeks of so much brimstone that I wonder if the Devil himself has paid a visit.

There is even more straw on the floor now than when I first arrived. It's as if these crates magically generate more and more packing material.

Disappointingly, the tenant is not here. I was looking forward to thanking him for his remedy, but now my gratitude has nowhere to land. I call out, but there is no answer. I try the vacant room. It is still empty, but now there are more puzzling symbols chalked all over the walls. I try the second room, but the door will not open. What is in here that requires a lock? I am like a cat in that way, unable to abide the mystery of a closed door. I jiggle the handle and bump the wood with my shoulder.

"Don't go in there," says the voice behind me.

Victor stands in the entrance, looking very much like a wastrel. His clothes are damp and disheveled, his hair wild as if tossed by the winds.

"Good Lord," I declare. "What happened? Are you all right?"

He drops onto the bench with an exhausted sigh. "I went for a walk."

"Did you fall in? You're soaked through."

He peels off the jacket and hurls it onto the cot. "It rained last night," he says. When he registers my puzzled expression, he elaborates. "My humors are never in balance. I brood. One of my many faults, you see."

"We all have faults, sir. You're not remarkable in that."

"Victor," he says.

"Beg your pardon?"

"Don't call me sir. I'd like to think we are on friendlier terms than servant and master."

There is a bottle of dark glass on the table. I watch him pour some into a cup. My first instinct is to tut-tut this tipple, but who am I to scold. He's a grown man, isn't he? I survey the disaster of the leased cottage.

"I see you've been busy," I say. I brush a new stain on the wall, but the strange soot is etched deep. "If you're not careful, you're going to burn the place down."

He sips the cup. "I get carried away. I seem to have only two modes of conduct these days. I am either working feverishly or I sit dejected and brood. I prefer to be busy."

"You need to learn moderation," I tell him. "Candles that burn at both ends don't last very long."

The bottle tips again. He slides a cup across to me. "Have some wine."

"You should eat something." I place his meal before him and remove the cloth. "Have you even slept?"

He takes up the spoon. "I will eat, you will drink. Fair trade?"

Wine is a rarity in our home. It is a tart, but pleasant treat, nonetheless. When I start to tidy up, he tells me to stop. Sit and talk, he pleads. I thank him for his powders, and he is happy to hear that little Effie is doing better. He asks me about the other children; how old they are and what they are like. What parent doesn't enjoy talking about their children? He asks about Mr Tulloch and how long I have lived on Eynhallow. Where I am from. I relay facts without embellishment or color. I find myself bored by my own history. His questions tack a little deeper, asking about my height. Was I tall as a child or did it come on suddenly? What about the slight curve in my spine? He asks odd questions about my strength and about my monthly turns. Were any of my children difficult births?

I should take offense at these intimacies, but I do not. It is strange being the focus of so much interest that is not mockery. It is not unpleasant, mind you. I am simply not used to it. He's particularly interested in the growth spurt I experienced that resulted in my stature. How painful my limbs ached and how my life changed after that. How I was often the target of mockery or derision. He asks if I worry about any of the children inheriting this same affliction. I am taken aback at that one. How did he know? Grace is twelve. I am dreadfully afraid that she will endure the same experience when she reaches her next birthday. He asks if I ever take ill. I have to stop and think about it, but no. I can't remember the last time I was sick. I tell him about the birth of my seven children. Three lost, he surmises correctly. The only birth that was difficult was the first. He was born blue, and I did not name him. The other births were fine. Two of them did not last their first three months, but I remain grateful that four have lived. I think about the lost ones all the time, but I rarely speak of them. Discussing them now, so frankly and out in the open, brings on an abrupt mistiness to my eyes.

"Forgive me," he says. "I have an overactive curiosity. It outruns my manners at times."

I dry my eyes and the conversation turns to lighter fare. He asks about the post. How often it arrives and who on the island receives it.

"Mr. Dearness is our postmaster," I tell him. "If he is not around, they bring it to Mr. Heddle."

He looks into his cup as if there is something more than wine dregs to be found there. "I see."

"Are you expecting something?"

"I've arranged for a delivery to come from Edinburgh," he says. "They said they would notify by letter before it is shipped."

"Edinburgh? From the college you visited?"

He nods. "It is an element vital to my work, and I am anxious for its arrival."

Sounds very important. When I ask what it is, he says it is a certain material he needs to continue.

"Everything depends on it," he says. "Even my very happiness."

I ask what could possibly be so important, but he dismisses it, explaining that he gets carried away sometimes. I don't press the matter, but he is not a very good liar, this Victor Frankenstein.

CHAPTER XIII

Another Sunday, another service among the ancient ruins. The wind is strong this day, stealing away Mr. Dearness' words before they reach us. The result is the same as our gospel reader never makes sense anyway. His silvery hair whips about his head as he reads, giving him the comical aspect of an aged gorgon.

The new tenant's absence from church is again noted by all and is the choke point of discussion in the post-service chatter. By now, everyone knows that I am cooking for the infidel at the haunted croft. On a normal Sunday, Nelly Heddle and Mary Dearness want little to do with me, but they corner me now, eager to peck at me for scandalous details. They want to know what he's like. Is he mad? Is he dangerous? Is he an exile fleeing some scandal on the continent?

"Nothing so dramatic," I tell them. "He's a student of the sciences. He's come here to work."

This satisfies neither of them. They're hungry for some scrap of gossip, something bloody.

"Well, that hardly makes sense," tuts Mary. "Why come here for that?"

Nelly agrees. "There must be more to it. Is he on the run from bad debts or an indiscretion with some Jezebel? You're his washerwoman, Agnes. You must know more."

I find my neighbors tiresome at the best of times. Today, I despise how they swarm like flies on a dung heap.

"I am not his servant," I tell them. "And there is little else to tell. He works, he sleeps. He barely speaks when I'm there."

They keep digging and I keep dodging. They are convinced the new tenant is corrupt and desperately want something from me to support their baseless suspicions. I find myself defending his character at their timid attempts to slander the man. Excusing myself from their claws, I gather the children and leave. I am surprised at how irked I am by this exchange. Is it just my dislike of these two ninnies or is there something more to it? It is no skin off my nose if the women shred the man behind closed doors.

The tenant at Merryman croft is prone to volatile temperaments. One day he is exultant over progress in his mysterious work, and other days I find him dejected and sulking over a setback. It is the latter state that I find him when I return to the cottage this evening. He is sitting on the floor among all that damn straw, tossing pebbles into an upturned hat. He doesn't even look up when I enter.

"Another setback?" I ask.

"It is nothing but setbacks," he grumbles. "This whole infernal process. It is ugly and repellent in its very nature. I should quit. Run away. Hurl myself off the cliff."

"You can't do that, Victor."

His look is sharp. "Why not?"

"What would I do with my evenings now?" This fails to elicit a smile. He goes back to tossing pebbles, so I try a different tactic. "Why don't you tell me about yourself. Where are you from? What is your family like?"

"There is nothing to tell," he says.

"Oh, stop sulking. You've asked endless questions about me. It's only fair. I really know very little about you."

He leans his head back against the wall. "I am by birth a Genevese; and my family is one of the most esteemed of that region."

"A nobleman," I say.

"My father is," he says. "I have yet to distinguish myself in any commensurate way."

I take a seat on the bench. "You still have time to make your mark on the world."

He laughs at this remark, but not in a pleasant way. I ask about his family, and he tells me of his father, a magistrate from a long line of magistrates. He has two younger brothers, Ernest and William, and he has a cousin, Elizabeth, whom his family has fostered since she was five years old. The girl's family had met with misfortune and Victor's mother rescued the poor child from a life of certain misery. I ask what this Elizabeth is like and how old she is.

"She is a good person with a kind heart," he says, but he seems reluctant to discuss her.

"And are she and your mother close?"

56

"My mother is dead," he says. "Elizabeth came down with scarlet fever when she was young. Mother nursed her, of course, but the fever took her."

"I am so sorry. How old were you when this happened?"

"Seventeen," he says. He looks up at me. "You haven't told me about your mother. What is she like?"

"She is also passed. Bronze John took her when I was six."

He is unfamiliar with that name. I describe her ailments and he identifies it as yellow fever. I am impressed at his knowledge.

"Are you also a physician?" I ask. "Is that part of your studies?"

"Not a qualified doctor, if that's what you mean. But I could pass for one, I suppose." He stretches out his legs, crossing one ankle over the other. "Was your mother a tall woman?"

"No. She stood the same as my father, but he is not a particularly tall man."

He ponders this for a moment. "Curious. So where do you suppose your height comes from?"

"I haven't a clue," I tell him. "There was this one cruel boy who lived next door to us. He spread a rumor that my mother secretly lay with a giant troll from the Norse lands, which explained my stature."

"What an odious pest. That must have been upsetting."

"It was, but more because of the slur against my mother," I remark. "When I discovered who was telling these lies, I boxed the boy's ears for it. He never spoke a word of it after that."

His laughter is bright, and it fills the cottage. He leaps to his feet and claps his hands in an abrupt change of mood. How mercurial the man is.

"Agnes," he says, "I need your help with my studies. Come, on your feet."

"I cannot help you with your sciences, Victor."

He gathers up his sketchbook and a stick of coal. "On the contrary, you are the only one who can help me. I've told you that anatomy is a foundational element of my work, yes? The secret mechanics behind muscles and bones, of arteries and circulation."

He is not making much sense. "I know nothing of these things."

"And yet you can teach me everything." He places a stool before the hearth and turns a lamp to its brightest glow. "Come here, where the light is strongest. I want to sketch you."

"I beg your pardon?"

His face beams, his eyes bright with anticipation. "I want to sketch your anatomy. The clockwork of muscles and the gears of joints. From every angle, if we have time. It is crucial."

My head is already shaking. "Don't be mad. I am no muse."

"Ah, but you are, sweet Agnes! Not a muse in the frothy artistic sense, but a muse of pure science. The most noble of muses. Good, yes? Now disrobe."

He backs away a few paces and turns the sketchbook to a fresh page. I get the sense that Victor is used to having his orders obeyed. He looks up, impatient that I have not shed a single stitch.

"Why do you tarry?" he asks. "Will you be too cold? I can put more peat on the fire."

Maybe the man really is mad. My fists plant on my hips. "You must be joking. I cannot disrobe for you."

"Not for me, Agnes," he exclaims. "It is for progress! For science! The highest of ambitions. Come now. Off with it all."

I refuse. He demands. The argument goes back and forth like this before he accepts that I will not be swayed. For all his knowledge and brilliance, he seems quite dunderheaded about how the world works.

"There is nothing prurient about this, Agnes. Nothing lurid or untoward. The human frame is a miracle of engineering and locomotion. A fusion of grace and practicality. And yours, with your height and strength, is more miracle than most. Please."

His arguments are reasonable, but my cheeks burn at the very idea of it. He snaps his fingers and runs to the windows to close the shutters against any peeping Thomas. Then he bolts the front door and returns to take up his paper and pencil.

"There. You are secure and safe. No one will know, but us." He waves his hand at me. "Now disrobe, please."

Every shred of my being is refusing to relent, and yet, my hands are already loosening buttons and untying lace. I feel lightheaded and strange. It is like I am looking down at myself as I toss aside the shawl, shrug out of the stays and loosen the petticoat until there is only the thin shift. This too slips away and falls to my feet, leaving me utterly defenseless. The room is silent save for the crackle of the fire and the scratch of pencil on paper.

CHAPTER XIV

Who have I become? This is not me. I am not a person of murky morals and reckless actions. I am quiet and obedient. I pray, I instruct my children to be good and upright in all things. And yet there I stood, as exposed as a newborn, letting a man, a man whom I barely know and is not my husband, render my portrait in a coal rubbing. Have I become Parisian overnight? Is this Victor's fault? Has he swayed me with his continental and licentious thinking?

The children are asleep when I return home as quiet as a thief. Mr. Tulloch is not here. He must be with George, tippling the water of life. No one is here to witness the crimson wash of guilt on my face, thank Christ.

Nothing catastrophic happened at the Merryman cottage. Victor instructed me on how to stand, where to place my limbs, and he made study after study in charcoal. He asked me to constrict my muscles to make them prominent on the flesh. He's a fair artist, rendering quite extraordinary specimens of arms and legs and torsos on the page. I asked to see them after I got dressed and was quite delighted with his work. It is a peculiar thing to see oneself through the eyes of another, as Victor had done with these studies. But this is more than simple portraiture here, for in many of these drawings, Victor has peeled back the flesh to expose the muscles beneath, the arterial tendrils that resemble roots winding around a limb. Some reveal the very bones beneath an arm or a foot. Seeing them was a baffling experience, as if seeing myself flayed away layer by layer.

There was one sketch that I kept coming back to. Not one of the gruesome drawings, but a simple head-and-shoulders portrait. I am not one to linger in the mirror—I am often disappointed in what I see in the glass—but what Victor had rendered was something altogether unexpected. The woman in the portrait is comely and pleasing to the eye. If I didn't know better, I would say the person in the drawing is a noblewoman. He must have thought me vain for how entranced I was by it. He tore the page from the book and told me to keep it.

"I have something else for you," he said as I tightened the lace on the stays. "I came across it yesterday. I don't know why I brought it, since it has no bearing on my studies."

From a stack of books on a side table, he selected a slim volume and placed it in my hand. The title on the opening leaf was stamped *The Sorrows of Young Werther*. Unlike the other books here, it was written in English.

"Add it to your library," he said.

On an earlier visit, I had snooped through the books that were stacked hither and thither throughout the cottage, but every volume was written in French, German, or Latin. Victor seemed amused by my interest in books. I explained that my father considered it vital that I become literate, and taught me himself. I adore reading, but the Tulloch cottage contains only three books. One is an almanac from 1793, and another is *Pamela, or Virtue Rewarded* by Richardson. The last volume is a Bible, of course. I have read all three more times than I care to remember. Having something new to read is like a dozen Christmas mornings! I thanked him and hurried home, for the hour had turned late.

The whole experience was exceedingly strange. When I first disrobed, I was awkward and terribly self conscious, but the artist went out of his way to put me at ease with his instructions and kind words. His compliments, even. I soon relaxed, feeling neither guilt nor shame while he worked, and I left the croft delighted with the book he had given me. It is not until the pathway leads me home that my stomach begins to roil and flip with bad feelings. It is as if a pitcher of unkind emotion has been poured down my gullet and stirred violently to make me sick.

Thank God the children are asleep, and Mr. Tulloch absent as I creep inside. A single glance from any of them and I would confess the whole thing.

I keep telling myself that I have done nothing wrong, but I am restless and the tension in my nerves is cranked tighter than a drum. I remember the book. Bringing the lamp a little closer, I curl up in a chair to read. I slip into the world of this young man, Werther, as easily and deliciously as one slips into a hot bath. How delightful it is to have some new world to visit, for the chance to walk in the steps of someone other than myself. I even stop to reread a few lines just for the joy of them. Like this bonny tidbit; "misunderstandings and neglect occasion more mischief in the world than any malice and wickedness." I nod in agreement and read on. How I envy the person who can distill thoughts and emotions into words on a page. It is magic.

The door bangs open, ruining everything. Mr. Tulloch has returned and, as I suspected, he's been at the Heddle croft. He is clumsy with drink and overly loud for this hour.

"Hush, Robert," I whisper. "The children are asleep."

"Oh yes, the children." He stands there, blinking at me. "We mustn't disturb the wee angels."

He's in a mood. How wonderful. He bumps the table, causing a cup to rattle. He puts a finger to his lips and oafishly shushes himself. I should have gone to bed before he staggered home. It is always a gamble as to his mood when he's in this state. Some nights he is in high spirits and wants to chat, to dance a jig, but most nights his humors run dark. He can be argumentative or nitpicking, criticizing everything I do or say. Some nights he is libidinous and wants to rut. The worst of all are the nights when he is overwhelmed with self pity. *Look at my life*, he'll sob. *What have I done to deserve this?* he'll moan. *All I do is toil, and for what? Is there any thanks?*

He hasn't revealed his mood yet. He regards me with a dark look, swaying a little. Then he strikes, quick as a viper, snatching the book from my hand.

"What in the name of Job is this?" He flips through its pages, not a word of which he can read. When asked to sign a deed, Mr. Tulloch simply scribes an X.

"It's just a book," I tell him. "Don't be rough with it."

"Ooh, a book you say? Do ye think I don't know what it is, Agnes? Am I too thick to understand what this object is? Too much the peasant? Is that what you're implying, my saucy girl?"

This is not our first row on this subject. He resents the fact that I know letters and he does not. When he's in a cruel mood, he often mocks me for it. Being illiterate is unfortunate, but it is nothing to be ashamed of because it is so common. I was extremely fortunate to have been taught when I was younger, and I do not begrudge Mr. Tulloch the fact that letters frustrate him. The same cannot be said for his position. Early on in our marriage, I made the mistake of offering to teach him. He reacted like I had threatened to burn the cottage down. His lid almost popped off his skull, so vexed and outraged he was. Lesson learned; I have never mentioned it again.

He asks where I got the book and I watch his face darken when he learns its origin. The volume lands in the fire.

I burn my hand trying to save it. His boot goes into my back. Like our other quarrels, this is not our first violent jig. I am taller than Mr. Tulloch, and stronger by far, but I do not fight back. I cannot. One trait that I possess is an almost unhealthy tolerance for pain, so I cover my head and take the blows until he tires himself out. I wait for the signal that concludes every such dance as this. And there it is. He spits on me. A wet smack on the hand covering my head, my hair.

Mr. Tulloch flops into the chair, wheezing from his exertions. I get to my feet, undress, and go to bed.

CHAPTER XV

There is no mention of the incident this morning. Mr. Tulloch wakes and goes about his duties like every other dreary day. I doubt he even remembers what he did. My lips are pursed tight, letting nothing slip. My back is sore and my lip is split, but I keep my mouth closed. What is there to say? It is the way of things, and it has always been the way of things. When he finally goes out the door, I let out a very long breath. The peace does not last long as the children become calamitous and somehow Daisy the goat has found her way inside. She munches happily on a sack of oats until I take her horns and steer the mischievous animal outside. Meg calls me cruel and chases after her pet.

Cruelty. It blooms behind closed doors like mold, thriving in places where sunlight doesn't reach. It festers in the clenched jaw until it rots a molar. Ours is not a happy union, and yet my husband and I go to great lengths to pull the wool over every eye and publicly present the very idyll of matrimonial union. Why? I do not know. Is anyone on the isle fooled by our mummer act? I doubt it. And yet we go on, pantomiming like clowns before the footlights.

Why do I put up with it? Why do I not flee? And go where? Who would shelter a woman with four babes in tow? Certainly not my father. The shame of it would be too much. Besides, once my stepmother had married me off, she bolted the doors and drew up the drawbridge against her unsightly stepchild. As a mother who abandons her marriage, I would have few options; begging on the streets or placing myself and my children in the workhouse. I suppose I could be a three-penny-upright, but the clientele would need a stepladder.

I decide to visit Katie. Her wit and disposition are the perfect foil to my brooding, so I round up my little barbarians and lead them along the coast path to the Kemp farm. Thomas looks positively relieved when he answers the door. He lets us in, whispers something to me about the ma'am being in a mood and slips away. Katie is indeed not faring well. Her stinging back will not let her sleep and the weariness droops her pretty features like a damp veil. She waddles about, refusing to sit or rest.

"Sitting only makes everything hurt," she says.

The days before birth can be the most trying. Meg would not let me catch a wink, constantly kicking and squirming about in my belly. It was like she was already fighting with her brother from inside the womb. I do what I can to make Katie comfortable, but there's more than an aching back and constant piddling that is troubling my friend. The air inside the cottage is strained when I arrive, but it eases when her husband leaves.

"Trouble with Tom?" I ask. "Is he not taking care of you?"

Katie takes the bread I've brought her and slices pieces for the children. "He's fussing over me well enough. He just won't listen to me."

Common enough, with or without a swollen belly. "About the babe?"

"There's something here, Agnes." She looks out the dusty window to the heath beyond. "Something is on the isle with us."

The children, both my brood and hers, stop chewing and look up. Like rabbits, their ears twitch and crane at the hint of anything not meant for them.

"Outside, all of you," I declare with a clap of my hands. I make sure each child has a hunk of bread and shepherd them out the door. Tragically, there is nothing left for the one person who needs it. Katie wets a finger and collects the crumbs from the table. With the coast clear, I return to the topic at hand. "What do you mean, something is with us?"

She leans in close, even though we are alone in the cottage. "I saw something early this morning that gave me such a fright I thought the babe would drop."

"What was it?"

"I'm not sure. It was still dark, just before daybreak. But I saw this...thing... lurching out on the shore." She shakes her head at the memory as if to loosen it from her brains. "I don't think it was human."

I hold my breath. My mind immediately recalls the dark shape I saw a week ago, but I keep that to myself for now. I am also mindful not to dismiss her fears. Clearly her husband has, which explains the tension between she and Tom.

"Can you describe it? This thing you saw?"

Her gaze turns from the window to me. "You don't think I sound mad?"

"No. You sound scared. Tell me about it. What did it look like?"

Katie sighs, folds her hands in her lap. "It was gigantic. In fact, it was so tall I first thought it was you. But that was silly. Why would you be skulking the beach at dawn?"

Tim McGregor

There's no need to ask Katie why she was outdoors at such an hour. The baby won't let her sleep, so she went to get some air.

"What else about it?" I ask. "Did you see its face? Or any features?"

She shakes her head. "It was too dark. All I saw was its shape. But the size of it, and the way it moved. No normal person ambulates like that."

The fear in Katie's eyes rings true. Regardless of what this thing was, it has truly scared my friend. I take her hand. How swollen her knuckles have become. "What do you think it was?"

"Do you think the stories are true? About trolls hiding in caves? I always thought they were ghost tales to frighten children, but what if they exist? What if that is what I saw?"

"I don't know," is my reply. "Is it possible your eyes deceived you? The poor light was playing tricks?"

Listen to me, being as dismissive as a man. What she describes matches the thing I also saw, so why am I brushing aside her concerns? I don't want to alarm Katie by revealing my own sighting, but silence feels like a betrayal.

Katie holds her head in her hands. "I don't know what to think. My head is in such a fog these days. This baby is not content with eating my supper, it is stealing my brains also."

The poor thing needs rest. I ask if she wants a dram, it might help her sleep, but she declines. I don't know how to help her.

"Have you eaten?"

"I'm not hungry."

"You need to eat, Katie. Sit tight. I'll fix something."

The conversation tumbles to more mundane topics, such as the children, the weather. I make a trifle joke about Nelly Heddle's weasel face, which makes my friend laugh. In the end, I decide not to tell Katie of the misshapen thing I saw on the shore. She has enough to worry about and scaring her would just rob her of more sleep now.

She nibbles on the bit of herring I've made her and sighs. "Sorry to have made such a fuss," she says. "I am really not myself these days."

"The last stretch is hard. I remember with Effie, Robert and I fought like the devil before she came."

Katie laughs at this, but then stops when she sees my face. There are times when I can hold it all in and other times I cannot. My mask slips now and my distressed friend is asking me what the trouble is. I tell her it's nothing, but Katie hates that answer.

65

"Out with it," she insists.

I shrug, like it is not worth mentioning. "Another row, that's all."

Her expression flattens out. "I see. Is that how your lip was split?"

I nod. I shrug.

"What was it about this time?"

"A book, of all things. Can you imagine?"

She asks how rough it got. I lie and tell her it was a minor skirmish. She rubs my back. Am I not supposed to be comforting her? How did I get this so turned around? Katie slips her arm through mine, and we sit and gaze out the door for a moment.

"You know, you can always come here," she says. "Before the row gets out of hand like that, step away and come stay with us. You're always welcome."

"And leave the children behind?"

She looks down, brushes a crumb from her lap. There is no practical answer to this, so neither of us says anything.

"It's like he's two people," I say. "Jolly one day, a tyrant the next. I just wish he'd make up his mind about which one he is. It would make things easier." I feel I am about to ramble for a bit. "He never used to be like that. Robert was kind and charming in the beginning."

Katie laughs. "They're always like that when courting. Once they've got you, they tend to get lazy."

I look at her. "Tom's not like that. He's always good to you."

Katie can't really argue this. She shrugs at me. "He blows wind a lot. Try living with that."

My friend has a knack for cracking open the absurd side of things to make me laugh. God, what would I do without her?

Both of our spirits have lifted a little by the time I corral the children home, so I consider that a small victory. There are so very few of them, and I must cherish the ones I get. The children run and caterwaul all the way home. Daisy scampers along with them, never far from Meg's side. I am surprised to find a visitor waiting outside my door. Hugh Dearness halloes as I draw near. There is a letter in his hand.

"Good morning, Mr. Dearness. How are you?"

"Well enough, Agnes," he says. His face is a little flushed from the walk uphill. "I see you're coming from Tom's croft. How is our Mrs. Kemp? Has the babe come?"

"Any day now. Katie is having her patience tested with this one." I nod at the letter in his hand. "Is that for Mr. Tulloch?"

Mr. Tulloch does not correspond with anyone and thus, never receives letters. It must be from the laird, then. Which can only mean bad news.

"No, this is addressed to the tenant at Merryman's." He hands the letter to me. "Will you be a dear and deliver this for me?"

"If you wish. I'm sure he's home if you want to deliver it yourself."

He waves the notion away. "The less I have to do with that heathen, the better. Thank you, Agnes."

The old goat. Aside from his dislike of the godless foreigner, I have a suspicion that the spectral reputation of the deserted croft has something to do with Mr. Dearness' reluctance. A thought occurs to me as he turns to go.

"Mr. Dearness, may I ask something? Have you seen anyone skulking about late at night? Or early in the morning, near dawn?"

His brow wrinkles. "What do you mean, dear? I've seen Mr. Tulloch stumble home late from the Heddles a time or two if that's what you're referring to."

"No, I mean a stranger. Not one of us. And not the new tenant, either."

His slight shoulders lift and drop. "There is no one else. Why?"

"Oh, no reason." I brandish the letter in my hand. "I'll deliver this to Mr. Frankenstein today."

Mr. Dearness rolls his rheumy eyes. "That name."

I watch him totter down the dirt path. Mr. Dearness' eyesight is quite poor, and I doubt he'd notice anything unless it was hard up against his nose, let alone a figure in the dark. I am still a little unsettled by Katie's sightings and even more by her words. How did she put it?

Something is on the island with us.

CHAPTER XVI

I find the tenant asleep at the table, with a riot of diagrams for a pillow. Shaking him gently, the man startles awake like one expecting an assassin. He's on his feet, brandishing the poker until his frighted eyes take in his situation. He apologizes for his outburst.

"You have to stop working through the night," I tell him, gathering up the notes scattered by his fit. "You are going to wear yourself out like this."

He grumbles something unintelligible and goes to the wash basin to splash cold water over his face. I stir the fire to life and hook the kettle on the peg. Among the strange ampules and bizarre instruments the new tenant brought with him, there is also a rare commodity that he says is crucial to his work. Coffee. He showed me how to use the small grinder to pulverize the beans and prepare a pot of the dark restorative. I tried a little, but found it too bitter for my taste.

I set the cup before him, and a few sips are enough to revive him. "Thank you, Agnes," he says. "You are a godsend."

"I don't like seeing you exhaust yourself, Victor. What good is that brilliant mind of yours if it housed in a broken vessel?"

His eyes harden through the vapors of the cup. "I had such terrible dreams."

"Oh?" I reply. I rarely remember my own dreams. "What did you dream of?"

"My mother," he says. "I dreamed she was here, banging on the door and demanding to be let in. I was terrified to open it, but I seemed unable to stop myself. There she stood, draped in her funeral shroud and reeking of the grave. Worms crawled through the folds of the funeral cloth and her lips had rotted off, exposing the teeth. She wanted to warn me of something terrible, but with no lips or tongue, all she could utter was this terrible clucking sound."

How ghastly. "That sounds awful. What was she like, your mother?"

"She was a kind woman with an overly charitable heart," he says. "She wanted to save everyone."

"Overly charitable? You said the fever took her?"

He sips the coffee, nods. "She caught it nursing Elizabeth back to health."

"How sad." I brush soot from my sleeve. "And Elizabeth, she is your cousin, yes?"

"Not a true one. My mother took her in when she was a child."

"You were raised together? Sounds more like sister than cousin. Tell me more about your Elizabeth."

Hearing no reply, I look up. His eyes are shiny, the gaze running far from this place. Have I upset him somehow? "Victor? Are you unwell?"

His gaze snaps back to this place, this time. "Sorry," he says. "I keep seeing that awful dream of my mother."

"It sounds unpleasant." I straighten the bedlam of papers and notes on the table. "What terrible warning do you think she wanted to impart?"

The spoon tinkles the china as he stirs his cup. "It doesn't matter. Dreams don't mean anything."

"Well, maybe this will dispel the bad dreams." I produce the letter and set it before him. "It arrived this morning."

He tears it open, scans it quickly and leaps to his feet. I cannot tell if it is good news or bad until he flings the letter high and embraces me. He dances me around the room like a lunatic.

"Good news?"

"The best news!" he cries, spinning me about.

It is an awkward dance as his eyes meet my collarbone and my feet are clumsy. I am happy for whatever good fortune has come his way, but the intimacy of this dance is uncomfortable. Things are stirred up and my thoughts tack to improper winds, so I back off. I beg him to share his good news.

"The delivery from Edinburgh," he grins. "The one vital resource I need to finish my work. It is waiting for me on the mainland."

I clap my hands. "Congratulations, then."

"You've no idea what this means, Agnes," he says. There is a strange and hungry light to his eyes. "I can now complete my work and fulfill my obligation. Then I'm free. Free of this wretched curse!"

"Curse?" I reply. Has the man lost his wits? "What on earth do you mean?"

"Nothing, nothing," he says, retrieving the letter from the floor. He scans it again. "Do you know where Tingwall dock is?"

"It's a small port on the coast, just south of here. May I see the letter?"

He hands it to me and folds his arms, deep in thought. "I'll need to hire a boat to go fetch it. Who on the island has a boat I can lease for a day?"

"Everyone," I tell him. "Robert has a good boat. Sturdy."

I scan the short dispatch. It is from the porter at Tingwall dock, saying a crate has been delivered from the Edinburgh Anatomical School for Mr. V. Frankenstein of Eynhallow. It will be held for one week's time. After that, a holding fee will be applied until collection is made.

"Excellent," Victor declares. "And Mr. Tulloch will let me utilize his boat for a day? I'll pay him a good fee for it."

"Mr. Tulloch will let you do anything for a good fee." My temper is still hot from last evening and I cannot resist being petty. "But don't go alone, Victor. Let Mr. Tulloch take you to Tingwall. It's dangerous."

He digs into a pocket and counts the coins there. "I know how to navigate a rowboat, Agnes. Besides, I need a certain degree of discretion here."

"The current runs swift between here and the mainland. It looks passable enough, but it can be treacherous. Hire Mr. Tulloch to take you. Please."

The tenant turns to the table and digs through the mess of papers and books. "Very well. I appreciate the concern."

I say goodbye, needing to return home before my children burn the croft to the ground. I pause at the door. "Victor, may I ask you something?"

"Of course, of course," he says, digging through documents.

"I do not mean to pry, but are you in some kind of trouble?" I ask. "What wretched curse do you refer to?"

He ceases rummaging and looks at me. "It is nothing. I sometimes make the melodrama when my blood is up."

"I see," I tell him, but I do not necessarily believe him. I should leave it at that, but my mouth keeps trundling along. "If you were knotted in some kind of trouble, you can share that with me. I am good at keeping secrets."

He stops again. His expression alters for a moment, as if taken aback at my concern. "Thank you, Agnes. You are a very kind soul. A good friend, yes?"

"Indeed." I bid him farewell and hurry along before my cheeks redden.

The rest of the day passes in unremarkable drudgery. It is impossible to mind the children at all times and it is unfair of me to expect Grace to always herd her siblings like a good shepherd. Trouble finds its way no matter what. From outside the cottage comes a cry so shrill that I burn my hand on the iron pot. Vexed, I step out to find Kit and Meg fighting again. I do not understand why these two torment each other so, but what I witness as I round the corner stops my heart cold.

My only boy smacks his sister so hard she lands on her rump. He shrieks at her to mind her place and smacks her again before I can stop him. I yank the lad clean off his feet, dangling him by the offending hand.

"Stop it, Christopher! Don't you ever strike your sister!"

"But she deserved it," he cries, trying to wriggle free. "She's got a smart mouth and forgets her place!"

My temperature is boiling. Meg is crying, and that is no small thing. The girl never cries, no matter how bad it hurts. She has inherited her pain tolerance from me, no doubt. But she cries now, more from humiliation than pain.

"Forgets her place? Have you lost your wits?" I shake him. The lad jiggles like a broken puppet and I must be careful. "You do not strike your sister like that. Ever!"

The boy is stubborn. "She's mean! No girl should talk to me like that! She needs to learn her lesson!"

The violence is infectious, and it bubbles over in me. I smack his cheek so hard he sprawls on the ground, shock spilling across his face. Now the tears.

"In the house. Now!" I bark and point at the door. "Stay there until I tell you to come out!"

The boy runs. Not into the cottage, but clear across the turf to the other end of the island. I do not call after him. Meg's tears have stopped, but even she is a little shocked at what has transpired. I am not the parent with the quick hand. That is their father's role, and I feel like I have broken some unspoken agreement with my own children.

I loathe losing my temper. The boy's words have me seeing red, and yet my anger is misdirected. Kit is just a child aping what he has learned. My anger should be directed at his teacher in this regard.

The mentor in question appears a few minutes later, asking why he saw the lad run screaming across the isle like a devil. I tell him why, but Mr. Tulloch shrugs and sees no issue with the incident. My blood heats up again, but a stray thought is nagging me.

"Are you back from the mainland so soon?"

He looks confused. "Why would I go to Mainland today? It's not the first of the month."

"Didn't the new tenant come find you? He needs you to take him to port."

"He found me all right," Mr. Tulloch says. "He paid to borrow the boat. Said he wanted to row up the shore a bit and explore the island."

Producing a coin from his pocket, my husband makes a dimwitted jest about fleecing the foreigner and toddles off in the direction of the Heddle farm. My hands are suddenly cold as I reckon the transaction between the two men.

Good Lord, Victor. What have you done?

CHAPTER XVII

Leaving Grace in charge of the croft, I race across the heath, past the ruins, to the southwestern shore. Mainland looks deceptively close but the current that flows between us is fierce. For the most part it runs in a southerly direction, which means Victor would have crossed it in the rowboat easily enough and let the current ferry him down the coast to the dock at Tingwall. But getting home again is where the challenge lies. I scan the water and the far shore but see no boat. The sky is darkening, and the winds blow harder by the minute. The reckless oarsman will have to fight both current and a strong headwind to make his way back to Eynhallow.

I sit and wait, watching for a sign. Am I too late? Has the small craft already capsized, dragging Victor's body to the kelp bed? Perhaps the man has chosen a more cautious tactic, staying the night in Tingwall before attempting the route home. There is no inn, but someone would shelter the man rather than let him shiver in the elements all night. I can only pray that Victor will be sensible, but his temperament is so hot-headed that I fear for the worst.

An hour passes before I spy a little dot on the water, heading upland from Tingwall dock. It is Victor, rowing close to shore as he maneuvers up the mainland coast. I wish I had Mr. Dearness' spyglass, but even at this distance I can see him struggle. He makes progress, clinging to the shoreline to stay out of the current between us. As he gets closer, I spot an enormous crate crowded into that small craft.

Oh, be careful, Victor. That crate is not ballast. It is making the boat top-heavy and unsteady.

The craft comes parallel to Eynhallow and then Victor attempts to row straight across. The current claws him away south where the skiff bobs in the chop and spins him around. He puts his back into it, straining against the current, but his timing could not be worse. The wind lashes harder and now comes the rain. The chop rocks the little boat so fiercely I fear it will roll. I watch him push on, and he is almost across when a hard wave slams his side. The crate topples over and Victor lunges to catch it before it goes over, but the hull rolls under his feet and the skiff capsizes. The crate sinks and the boat upends. I cannot see Victor. Has he gone under? I pace the shore, calling his name, but the wind drowns me out.

There, flailing in the white chop, is the man.

My shoes are off, the heavy skirt dropped away. The sea is cold, and my clothes drag, but I keep swimming. The taste of saltwater burns my throat. The moment I seize the floundering man, he tries to climb up me to get out of the water, pushing me down into the darkness. I tear him off and break the surface before he drowns us both. I snatch the back of his collar and drag the idiot back to shore. When my feet find solid purchase, I haul Victor onto dry land and let him drop. A few thumps to his back and he spews up all the sea water he's swallowed. He lives. Taking his arm, I throw his limp body over my shoulder and ferry him home to my cottage where the fire in the hearth will revive him.

The fool. His precious cargo is now at the bottom of the sea and Mr. Tulloch's skiff will wash up on some Danish shore.

The children startle at the sight of their mother, soaked to the bone with a dead man over one shoulder. Their mouths drop when they see that it is the scandalous heathen from Merryman croft. I tell Grace to stoke the fire while I shake the drowned man, tweaking his cheek to rouse him.

"Victor, wake up. Open your eyes now."

His head bobs lazily, the eyes rolling open like a drunkard's. "Elizabeth? Where am I?"

Elizabeth. The cousin or half-sister he told me about. I grip both of his ears and administer another shake. "Victor, look at me. You're in my home. You almost drowned. Do you understand?"

His gaze wheels about, unable to focus on any one thing. "Am I dead? I am so cold."

Grace and Meg crowd around me, fearful but curious. Effie wants to be picked up. Of my son, there is no sign.

"Mother, what happened?" asks Grace. "You are soaked to the skin."

My clothes drip everywhere, dragging me with the weight of seawater. Victor shivers like a kitten abandoned in the rain.

"Girls, I need a blanket. The good one from our bed. Hurry now." Both daughters hie off. I take Victor by the lapels and haul him to his feet. "You need to get out of these clothes, Victor, before you catch your death."

He's too fuddled to think straight, so I undo the buttons and peel the wet garments from him. He protests. I push his hands away and tug away the sopping clothes. The girls return with the blanket, and I wrap Victor in it. I tell them to wring the gentleman's things and hang them to dry before the hearth. Effie ceases her mewling and goes to help her sisters.

I take hold of Meg's shoulder. "Where is your brother?"

"Up in the loft," she says. "He's still sulking."

Another mistake I must amend, but there's no time. I ask Grace to boil some water and make our guest a toddy. She dithers, reminding me that father's spirits are not to be touched.

"Never mind your father right now," I reply. "We need to warm the man's blood before he catches his death. Go on."

Meg is still leery of the man in the chair. She hides behind my skirts, and notices how sopped the material is. "You need to get out of this before you catch cold, too," she says.

Effie pipes up. "Mother doesn't get sick."

I am still shivering, though. With the excitement settling out, the chill cuts straight through to my bones. "Run and fetch my clean shift, Meg. There's a good girl."

Moments later, our guest and I are both draped and huddled before the hearth. Our clothes hang from pegs, steaming as the fire dries them. The toddies have done their work to revive us. I am still sipping mine, but Victor has drained his. The flames ripple in his glassy, unblinking eyes.

"Where are your brains, Victor?" My nerves are raw, clipping short any sense of propriety. "I told you the current was too strong. And now Mr. Tulloch's skiff is lost."

His look is not friendly. "A boat. That's what you are concerned about?"

"Your life was also a concern, if you hadn't noticed."

I watch something flinch through his frame. He looks at me with a sullen degree of remorse. "I'm sorry. Thank you. I will reimburse your husband for his lost property."

The contrition pecks away at my irritation. I soften. "I am just grateful that you were spared. There was a moment when I thought you would drown us both."

He passes the cup to my eldest daughter and asks for more. She hurries to fulfill the request.

"I am grateful for your kindness, Agnes," he says. "But you should have let me drown. It would have solved everything."

"Don't talk like that, Victor. Life is too short to be so morose, for God's sakes. Don't you know that?"

His shoulders lift and fall in a quick shrug. "My cargo was lost. What point is left to make? I am cursed and fate will come to collect the bill."

I don't understand these dark broodings of his, but when I ask him to explain, he pulls the blanket tighter about his shoulders and refuses to elaborate. The children, farther from the fire, watch us with silent, observant eyes. Even Kit, leaning over the precipice of the loft edge, cannot stifle his curiosity over our guest.

CHAPTER XVIII

The ice in my veins breaks up, the blood flows again. Victor's teeth have stopped chattering, but his spirits remain low.

"I don't think I'll ever be warm again," he says.

"Would you like some more to drink?"

He holds up his empty cup. "Please, if there is any."

My eldest takes it and fills the cup from the pot warming on a bed of coals. She returns it with a tiny curtsy. Sweet girl.

"This really is fortifying," he says. "You must be Grace, yes?"

"I am, sir."

"Thank you, Grace. It's a pleasure to meet you." He turns to Meg, perched on a stool nearby. "And you must be Margaret. The goat rider?"

The girl giggles and shies away.

"Your mother has told me all about you," he says to the children. "Where is the little one? Euphemia."

Effie darts behind me. She is normally not so shy, but the tenant of Merryman cottage has gathered something of a reputation, I suppose.

"It's all right, Effie." I drag her out into the open. "Mr. Frankenstein is a gentleman. He won't bite."

"Let's have a look at you," he says, motioning the child closer. "You were the one who was ill, yes? Come, come."

The child is skittish and needs prodding. Victor looks the girl over, checking her eyes and gently probing her throat. When he asks her to stick out her tongue and moo like a cow, Effie giggles and scurries back to me.

Something changes in his eyes. The children have lifted his spirits. "She's doing well," he says.

"Thanks to you," I tell him. My cheeks were frostbitten a moment ago. Why are they hot now?

Victor looks around our small cottage. "And where is the boy? Where is Master Christopher?"

Kit watches from the loft. He smiles, despite himself.

"There you are," says Victor. "Won't you come down, sir, so we may be properly introduced?"

Kit rolls over the rafter and lands on the floor, the monkey. He pops up, tall and puffed before our guest. They shake hands.

"Pleasure to meet you, Christopher," Victor says. "You're the man of the house, yes? When your father's not here, of course."

This puffs out Kit's chest even more. "Yes, sir," the boy replies. "Happy to know you, Mister Frankenstein."

Victor pats the boy's shoulder. "And how old are you, sir? Twenty-one, is it?"

Kit laughs. "I am eight." He looks at me, then back to our guest. "Did you really lose father's skiff?"

"I did. Stupid of me. But not to worry. I'll pay Mr. Tulloch for his lost property."

The boy's forehead knits. "What happened?"

"I should have listened to your mother," Victor replies. "The current was too much, and the boat rolled under my feet. In fact, I would have drowned if your mother hadn't saved my life."

My son's eyes widen at this information. With a flash, his respect for me swells and whatever enmity lingers between us is healed.

"Mother is quite strong, you know," Kit blurts out. "She can lift nine stone right over her head!"

Our guest turns to me. "Is that true?"

"The lad embellishes."

Offended, Kit fires back. "No, I don't."

The two of them chat and soon the other three crowd around, enjoying the guest's attention. I would not have guessed this man to be overly fond of children, but he has a rapport with them that makes me wonder if he is a father himself.

"All right, you little goats," I tell them. "Let the man breathe."

The children withdraw, but not too far. I can't help smiling at our guest. "You're very good with children," I remark.

"Am I? I haven't given it much thought really."

I tug the blanket closer. "One might assume you are a father yourself."

"Yes, well," he says, looking into his cup.

Have I asked him this question already or did I simply assume the answer. "Do you have children?"

Victor looks surprised. "I told you. I am not married."

"The two don't always align. It's not unheard of for a man to sire children outside of matrimonial entanglements."

His features go flat. Whatever mirth was there is now gone. The brooding returns. "No," he says grimly. "I have sired no children."

Why am I provoking him? "I'm sorry. That was rude of me."

"It's a fair question," he says, waving the notion away. "I had a brother who was quite young. I enjoyed his company. Your little ones remind me of him."

The past tense catches me by surprise. "Had? Oh. I am so sorry, Victor."

"It was tragic," he says.

"Which brother was this? Ernest or William?"

"Young Will. He was such a bright young thing."

I cannot stifle the questions running along my tongue. "May I ask what happened? If that's too delicate, please ignore me."

"His life was taken."

My jaw hangs open.

Victor registers my shock and then looks away. "His own governess strangled him. She swung for it."

Good God, what have I done? My petty curiosity has cracked open a terrible tragedy in this man's life. I am no better than Nelly Heddle. A child, murdered. I cannot begin to fathom the depths of this man's pain.

"I'm sorry, Victor. Forgive me for prying."

He falls silent for a moment, his eyes glassing over in remembrance. "He was a lovely boy. About the same age as your Margaret."

That is puzzling. "There was a great difference in ages between you?"

"Indeed. William was something of a surprise to my parents. Mother fretted over his birth, given her years, but in the end, he was a blessing to them. To us all, in fact."

"They sound lovely, your parents."

He reflects on this. "Theirs was a very strong union. Something to be admired, to strive after."

"They must have loved each other very much," I remark. "Not every union is blessed so."

His look is sharp, an eyebrow raised to me. "Are you unhappy?"

"No." Why have I steered the conversation to this ragged edge? It cuts too close to the bone, and I need to navigate the chatter to safer waters before I say something stupid.

"Do you wish to have children?" I ask.

He watches the fire. "What man doesn't?"

"That doesn't sound very convincing, Victor. Children are a blessing." I pinch Effie's cheek. "Even when they're being scamps."

"I suppose."

"You don't agree?"

"Not all progeny are a blessing," he says. His gaze goes dark again. How whipsnap his moods are. "Sometimes one's issue can be a curse. They haunt you."

That word again. Is he speaking of himself? Does there exist some terrible rift between himself and his father? I opt for bluntness and ask him outright if this is the case.

"No, no," he says, quick to dispel the miscommunication. "I love my father. He is a good man."

Hoisted on his own petard. "Then you really don't know of what you speak, Victor. Being without issue, I mean."

He grins, but the expression holds neither mirth nor affection. "Are you going to roast me? You did save my life, remember."

"I just think it's sad that you have a grim outlook on parentage. It is a wonderful thing, but it is not easy. You have to teach as well as love, and there are many times when one fails. But one still cherishes their offspring, no matter what the circumstances."

I am unsure exactly whom I am addressing in this moment, my guest or myself. I find it difficult to think clearly when I am in this man's presence. What on earth is wrong with me?

"It's hard to imagine you failing your children," he says. "They are a delight."

My heart still stings a little from seeing Kit strike his sister earlier today. And my own violence in turn. How the boy seemed to think he was entitled to such violence. How do I unteach him this lesson?

Our guest asks me if I am all right. Now I am the one doing the brooding. I wave it away and get to my feet. I run my hands along the garments hanging before the fire.

"These are dry enough, I think." I fold them and place them in his lap. "We've tormented you enough tonight. There is a screen there, by the back bed. You can dress there."

"Of course," he says, a little surprised. He almost seems disappointed that I've announced his visit is over. Or am I imagining such a thing?

The man gets dressed and emerges from behind the screen. The children don't want him to leave, and this genuinely delights him. He says goodbye to each of them. His farewell to me is a trifle stiff and more than a little awkward. He seems unsure of where he stands. He thanks me again and adds that he will return in the morning to compensate Mr. Tulloch for his lost property. He leaves and Kit asks why I had to chase the man away so abruptly.

"We were all having such a nice time," he says.

The lad doesn't realize it, but he has answered his own question. I do not want Mr. Tulloch to come home and find his wife and children fawning over a strange man. I do not have the stomach for a closed hand this night.

CHAPTER XIX

Robert is livid when he learns about the loss of his skiff. He curses the foreigner for being reckless and he curses me also, as somehow this is all my fault for suggesting it to the stranger in the first place. Mr. Tulloch's ire is justified, if not the severity of his outburst. The lion's share of our subsistence derives from what my husband can harvest from the sea with his nets and traps. We are also, he makes sure to underscore for me, now trapped on Eynhallow with no means of gaining the mainland. He is correct on this matter, but when I suggest he can always ask George Heddle or Tom Kemp for help going to town, he blows up all over again.

"What kind of man would I be," he seethes, "to go begging to the neighbor like some pauper?"

"Pride is a sin," I remind him. "And an impracticality at this point."

He does not like this reply and informs me that my opinions overreach my station. He goes back to cursing Victor for being a dimwit and to cursing all Continentals in general. Effie, who is too young to gauge the temperature in the room, pipes up to say that the man with the funny accent is a very nice fellow. When Robert learns that I had brought the man here to thaw out, he erupts into another tirade.

"Another man in my house!" he spews at me. "A feckless foreigner no less. Have your brains fallen out of your head, Agnes? What will the neighbors think? What will they say about me, with you sneaking the bastard in here?"

My nerves are as raw as my patience is thin. "That is an ugly accusation."

"Aye, it is. But if you think that is distasteful, what do you think the others will say about it? They'll flay the pair of us behind our backs. Good God, woman."

On and on his ranting goes, keeping everyone awake late into the night. When I suggest he lower his voice so the children can sleep, his swift hand goes up to silence me. I square him dead in the eyes and offer my cheek. If that will satisfy his rage, then so be it. Do your worst. The Christian gesture throws his ire off balance, and he chooses to kick a stool instead. Before the hour is done, he wears himself out and flops into a chair. I am grateful that he is not in his cups tonight. That would have prolonged his tantrum to an unendurable degree.

No one goes to sleep happy.

The sun rises and we all slip back into our roles like the gears of a miserable clock. Mr. Tulloch is still irate. He refuses to even look at me and spends his day out in the yard, which suits me just fine. At the noon hour, I go to the door to call him in for his dinner only to see the new tenant trekking down the beaten path to our home. He stops at the gate to speak to my husband. For a moment, I fear that Robert's rage will return, and a donnybrook might ensue, but my fears are misplaced. Mr. Tulloch is deferential as the stranger speaks to him. I watch Victor produce a wallet from which he retrieves a number of pound notes and place these in Mr. Tulloch's itchy hand. The two men speak a little more, with Robert bowing and bowing again, and then Mr. Frankenstein turns and walks back uphill.

Mr. Tulloch steps inside, all but dancing a merry jig.

"Did the feckless foreigner compensate you for your dinghy?"

He grins like a cat with a mouthful of feathers. "He did the honorable thing. Nay, he did it double, I'd say."

According to Mr. Tulloch, the tenant asked what the cost was to replace the vessel. Robert slyly inflated the figure, which Victor paid without question. My husband is quite pleased with himself for fleecing the Genevan. He even goes so far as to suggest the man is a bit dull-headed when it comes to numbers. This is, of course, laughable considering the walls of Merryman cottage are festooned with arcane equations.

"Did he have anything else to say?" I inquire. "Is he ill from his dip?"

Careful there, Agnes.

"You have the day off, my dear," Mr. Tulloch informs me. "He said he didn't want to be disturbed."

"Did he say why?"

"Who gives a fig why? Be grateful you don't have trudge up to that grim place." He scans the cottage around him. "Maybe you can put that extra time into cleaning up this barn."

He leaves again. Which is for the best since I have an overwhelming urge to throw something at him.

The rest of the day grinds itself out without incident. Mr. Tulloch remains in high spirits, which is a relief to everyone under this roof. He even bounces Effie on his knee for a minute, making the child squeal with laughter. I'd be a monster if I frowned on this. All the children are desperate for his approval or a kind word, which is a rare and special boon in this house. Kit especially so, as he feels he never meets his father's expectations. There are so many giggles and smiles around the table that one might think it Christmastime. Later in the evening when the children are abed and the embers dull in the hearth, I retire with a queasy knot in my stomach.

Still in good spirits, Mr. Tulloch nudges up close and wants to couple. I tell him no. When he pouts, I remind him of his betrayal last time. Out come the excuses and the empty promises not to repeat such an act. I dig my heels in, which only makes him paw at me more. He is stubborn. I relent just to get some peace, but not without a warning.

"I'll brook no repeats of the last time. If you do, I will twist your ear right off your damned head."

He swears up and down and then the bed starts squeaking. I keep an ear tuned to his breathing in case he tries to break my trust again, but my thoughts drift away. They creep along the footpath to the haunted cottage near the cliff, where a lonely man sits in despair at his setback. I wonder what he is doing and what thoughts he has. I wonder why he wanted to be left alone today.

The squeaking picks up steam. I push Robert off, leaving him to grunt in frustration and aim a few harsh words in my direction. I roll over and close my eyes.

CHAPTER XX

I overthink things too much. Once seized upon, I find myself unable to let go of an idea until it consumes everything. Why did the tenant of Merryman want to be left alone yesterday? Have I done something to offend him? Is he so despondent over the loss of his precious cargo that he's withdrawn from all human contact? His brooding knows no limits. Is it possible he's swinging from the end of a rope inside that decrepit cottage right now?

Thrice I scold myself to stop fretting the issue, but that does little to cool my brow. The worrying thoughts tumble on and on until a new one bubbles up and stops me in my tracks. I miss talking to Victor. As simple as that, the truth of it spills out in all its ugliness and veracity. Shame bolts straight through me, so I trap the dirty thought like a mouse and smother it before anyone smells the awful truth. Because, God help me, it reeks.

The day concludes without incident and another begins under gloomy skies and the patter of rain on the thatch. Out come the receptacles to catch all the leaks. The day mills along at a slug's pace, fraying my nerves even more. The inclement weather keeps Mr. Tulloch home, and the man annoys me to no end being underfoot. Impatient with his nattering, I head to the shoreline despite the rain. I catch three crabs for the pot. The family grouses, complaining that they are tired of crab. Even Kit, with his bottomless stomach, is displeased with it, consuming only one serving. I ration my own, ensuring there is plenty to bring the lone tenant uphill.

When supper is finished, I lift the pot from where it warms on the hearth and make my way north. The rain stopped an hour ago, leaving the isle sopping, but fresher somehow. Daisy the silly goat follows me until I chase her back. The pathway is sloppy with mud and twice I lose my footing, almost spilling the man's dinner. A dozen paces before the old house, something pulls my eye toward the ground and leaves me stupefied. It is a footprint in the soggy earth but is unlike any print I've witnessed before. It is human in structure, but its size beggars all belief. The giant troll I saw weeks ago. The same that Katie spied, though no one believed her. When I place my right boot into its relief, my foot is dwarfed by it. But the mark of this great thing is not singular. There are more of them, leading straight to the haunted croft.

Racing ahead, I burst through the door without knocking. The inside of the cottage is gloomy, with only a single lamp burning.

"Victor? Victor, are you here?"

A low groan to my left. I take up the lamp to push back the shadows until I find the Genevan. There, slumped against the wall like a dead man. But he moves.

"Victor, what happened?"

He cowers at my approach, arms shielding his head as if expecting a blow. His clothes are rent, and a raw look of terror clouds his eyes. It takes a moment for him to recognize a friend and not a foe.

"Easy now." I try to hold him still. "What happened to you? Were you attacked?"

His voice is brittle and unsure. "Agnes? Thank God, it's you."

I pull him to his feet and lead him to a chair. "Up off the floor. There now. Sit. Are you hurt?"

He shakes his head, but I bring the lamp closer to find a trickle of blood running down his chin.

"Who did this to you?"

"It's nothing," he wheezes. "Go home now. You shouldn't be here."

I take his chin and force his eyes to mine. "Stop it. What happened here? Did someone assault you? Tell me."

Are those tears or a trick of the weak light? He wipes his hands down his face, releasing a pent-up sigh. "I am fine. One of my turns came on, that's all. A fit. I'm sorry."

Irked, I tell him to hold that thought while I light another lamp and add a brick of peat to the fire. With the warmer lighting, I take in the overturned furniture and broken glass on the floor. It's like a rutting bull had been set loose within the cottage.

"Are you telling me you tore the place to ribbons in some hysteric fit?"

He glances over the mess but seems absurdly oblivious to it. "My humors," he says. "I get carried away sometimes."

"Did you bloody your own lip, too? Honestly, Victor."

A little spittle on my thumb cleans the blood from his chin. I turn his head the other way to find bruising on his throat. Purple whorls that resemble fingerprints on the sensitive flesh. He pushes my hand aside and looks away.

Dropping to my knees, I take his hands in mine. "Why won't you tell me what happened? Something was here. Its damn footprints lead straight to your door."

I see his shoulders twitch before I hear the man's sobs. I stiffen at the sight, unused to seeing a man weep. I rub his back for a moment and then tell him to dry up now. I lead him to the table and set the pot before him. Find a spoon.

"Eat."

He pushes it away. "I cannot."

I slide it back. "It will settle you. Eat."

My bearing remains sharp until he picks up the spoon. I right the tumbled chairs and sweep the broken glass into a corner. When I return to the table, the pot is almost empty.

"Did you eat at all yesterday?"

He wipes a wrist across his mouth but does not reply. I stand and root through the bureau for something restorative. I return with the brandy and pour him a dram.

"There. Are you ready to tell me what happened? You were clearly assaulted with violence. By whom? And why?"

He wilts in the chair. "I am so tired."

"Victor!" The man jumps at my fist banging the table. "No more of your moods or precious fits. Be straight with me."

I pour another length of the brandy and watch him throw it back.

"I owe someone," he says.

"A debt? Surely you can pay it, Victor. Your purse seems bottomless."

"There is more than money on the balance sheet," he says.

My patience is reaching its limit. "Victor, for God's sakes, will you just be straight with me? What is it you owe? Does it have to do with your work? And who is this person who attacked you? Besides being a giant."

His gaze slides to the fire. "He is a devil."

More riddles. How I want to shake some sense into this obstinate man. He looks up, noting my frustration.

"I am sorry, Agnes. It is too horrific to speak of." He rubs the bridge of his nose. "I just want to be shed of it. I want to run away from it all."

I take his empty glass and pour a length for myself. It is bracing and hot on my throat. "Then run. Escape."

"He'll never stop hounding me. Not until I deliver what he demands."

"Then give him what he wants and be done with it."

Victor leans forward. "That is what I came here to do. But the cargo is lost. I cannot complete my work without it."

"The delivery from Edinburgh? Send for more."

He scoffs at the notion. "It is extremely difficult to procure. Who knows how long it will take? And I am already out of time."

"Can you not go to the authorities? There is no constable on the island, but there is a magistrate in Kirkwall."

"No!" He seizes both of my hands in his. "No one must know."

"But this person has followed you here. He is clearly violent and dangerous."

His grip tightens on my hands. "Agnes, I beg you, tell no one. He is only a danger to me."

He says the shame is too great to have exposed. Again, he begs my silence, but when I ask him to explain, he refuses.

"You are a very sweet woman, Agnes Tulloch," he says. "But I cannot burden you with my troubles."

"You are no burden. It pains me to see you suffer like this." His hands are cold and yet they burn. "I don't know why you won't let me help you."

"But you do help me," he says. "Every day. This existence would be intolerable without your company. In fact, I was quite despondent yesterday without your visit."

My flesh bristles at this. "You asked me not to come."

"I needed time to think." He shakes his head at his own actions and picks up the bottle. "Will you have another drink with me? Let us discuss something else. Anything."

The man's moodiness will be the death of me yet. He flits wildly from morose to cheery in the wink of an eye. He forbids any further talk of obligations or the mysterious footprints outside his door. He asks about my children and if Euphemia's condition has improved. He tells me about Geneva and his childhood there. He describes a villa overlooking a placid lake in summertime. He tells me a curious tale of witnessing a tree struck by lightning, and how it opened the possibilities of the universe to him. A dozen more things are unpacked, keeping the conversation frothy and free of dour topics.

Victor paces about as we speak. He says he feels restless. He says his hands are itchy and in need of employment.

"You could fetch the broom and clean," I suggest. "Look at this place."

He laughs at this. "You are hopeless. Tell me something about you, Agnes. Something unusual or different. Shock me."

"There is nothing shocking to tell." I refill both glasses. "I'm more interested in you. Tell me some secret, Monsieur Frankenstein. Something you've never told anyone."

He takes the glass offered to him. "You are a sly one, aren't you? I'll not fall for that trap, my friend."

Friend. A simple enough word. Then why does my flesh tingle when he addresses me with it? My cheeks are flushed. "Tell me about the first girl you loved. What was her name and what was the appeal?"

His pacing stops. Lines crease his brow. "Elizabeth."

A name he's mentioned before. "Your cousin?"

"Yes. Well, it's complicated."

"It always seems so at the time," I reply. "What makes it thorny for you?"

"We grew up under the same roof. In truth, she is more sister than cousin." He swirls the spirits in his glass. "When my mother brought her into our home, she presented the poor thing as a gift to me. *A pretty present for my Victor*, she'd said. Since then I have looked upon Elizabeth as mine—and mine alone—to love and cherish."

Complications indeed. "And she was your first love?"

He nods. "It was my mother's wish for us to be wed when the time came."

This sharpens my attention. I hadn't considered this, though it is foolish of me. "Of course. So you are engaged then?"

"Upon my return to Geneva," he says. His hand passes over the cluttered instruments and odd tools. "Once this madness is concluded."

"Congratulations, then." It takes a hard effort to keep my expression flat. It stings, although it has no right to. What a fool I am. I should leave.

The tenant props an elbow on the mantel, stewing in his usual dark vapors. He does not seem like a man happily betrothed. I need to leave now, but my tongue has other plans and tumbles out a stupid question.

"Are you unhappy with the arrangement?"

His chortle carries more gloom than mirth. He looks at me. "I must sound terribly ungrateful."

"No. It just seems you have some doubts about it."

"I am unsure who I am doing this for. To make my father happy? My mother, even though she is dead?" He laughs again, but with a cruel flicker to his eyes. "An arranged marriage to honor a dead mother. It sounds ludicrous."

The fire crackles. He is pacing again, waving his thoughts away. "Who was yours? The boy who broke your heart?"

"Jamie." The name is there before I even ponder the question. Why is that? "A pauper's son."

His eyebrow arcs high. "Therein lies a tale of woe. Tell me."

I am in no mood to unpack this old business, so I summarize it briefly. Victor listens intently, and then asks if the love-struck boy ever came to rescue me. I reply that he did not.

"Do you ever wish he had?"

"That is none of your business."

The game has fizzled of all appeal. Sensing this turn, the gentleman from Geneva resumes his pacing. Again, he says he is restless and his hands are idle. I suggest cards, but he scoffs at the idea. He suggests dancing a jig, but I dislike my clumsy stomping and hovering over a dance partner.

I try to swallow what bubbles to mind, but it comes out all the same. "Another sketch, perhaps? That seemed to make you happy last time."

"Excellent idea," he declares.

I have become brazen, not giving a thought to closing the shutters. Who have I become? I twist and shrug out of the stays and petticoats, the shift. The stockings are pitted with holes and desperately need mending. They join the other clothes folded neatly on the bench. The man has the sketchbook on his lap, the charcoal in hand, but he stares at me for long time.

A sudden panic laces through me like a pistol shot. "Is something wrong?"

"No, no," he says, shaking off the distraction. The charcoal touches the paper. "Hold that for a moment."

He runs me through a number of poses as he dashes off study after study. Some of the sketches are full height renderings at a distance while others are closer observations of a hand or the hip bones.

"Anatomy," he tells me, as if needing to justify his scrutiny.

I don't care. He tells me to raise my arm this way, to turn my head that way. He steps back to sketch, he moves in close to render something specific. His hand takes my arm and poses it a certain way. He grips my knee to position my leg another way. I am out of breath, though I am as still as stone. Two or three times our eyes engage directly, and something lurches inside me, frightening and hungry. When it happens a fourth time, he is very close. My eyes drop to his mouth, and I cannot breathe because I want to touch his lips. The red cut on his lower lip looks raw and an insane urge to kiss it better makes me dizzy. I almost let the impossible happen, but I panic and retreat. I mention how late the hour is and gather up my clothes.

"Agnes," he says quietly.

"Sir," is my reply.

And like that, everything snaps back into its proper place.

What is wrong with me? I turn away to hide my shame and shuffle back into my clothes. Victor slides the heavy sketchbook onto the table and asks if I would like another drink before I go. I do not. It is raining again. The fall of it patters against the murky windows.

"Agnes," Victor says, holding out my shawl to me. "What happens to the wages I pay you?"

What an odd question? "How do you mean?"

"It's been over a fortnight. You must have nestled up a tidy sum by now?"

"Mr. Tulloch takes the wages," I reply. "Women have no heads for figures, as he likes to remind me."

He nods. "I thought as much. One moment."

At the table, he flips open an ornate walnut box and asks for my hand. The coins are heavy in my palm, and though I may be curious, I do not glance at them, let alone count them.

"These are for you, and you alone. For your assistance and discretion." He folds my fingers over the coins. "Understand?"

"Thank you."

He opens the door and I drape the shawl over my head to shelter from the rain. The ground is muddy again, but I do not see any trace of the footprints from before. The new rain has washed them all away.

CHAPTER XXI

Poor Katie. She is so uncomfortable and sick to death of being with child, and yet the stubborn babe refuses to come. I go to check on her for the second time this day to find her waddling about in a very disagreeable mood. I have to scold her to lie on the bed so I can poke and prod for any hint of birthing, only to disappoint my friend that she will have to wait a little while yet.

I brew some tea to settle her. When her discomfort lifts a little, she becomes her usual self and thanks me. Seeing with clear eyes, she tells me I look different. Happy, she remarks.

"What secret are you keeping, girl? You're not ripe with child, too, are you?"

My face flushes hot, but my belly is a ball of ice. I am mortified by whatever mien I am exhibiting to the world. Katie laughs and calls me a silly turnip. She tries to excavate the reason for my stammering, but I refuse to budge. I cannot, even with her. A convenient excuse comes to mind, and I flee home before the woman gets her nails into me.

You stupid, stupid woman, Agnes!

Small mercies, I return to find an empty cottage. There is no one here to witness me flail about in self-loathing and confusion. Who have I become? Some trollop putting it about with her heart on her sleeve? Poor Katie, as distracted as she is with her pain, saw right through me. Saints in a rowboat.

Last night's encounter with Victor has rendered me lightheaded and garish. I cannot stop thinking about it nor can I stop scolding myself for my behavior. I have not felt this overwhelmed since I tumbled head over heels for the penniless Jamie Grieve. But I was little more than a child then. How on earth can this happen now? Those feelings should have died on the vine long ago, shouldn't they? I am no blushing girl. I am twenty-nine years old. A wife and mother to four children, no less. I cannot, will not, let my heart render me a simpering lovestruck idiot!

I dry my eyes and turn to the looking glass to find a puffy face. I immediately turn away. I do not know who this woman in the mirror is now. She is a stranger, fawning over some man she barely knows.

You must be careful now, Agnes. You must put these feelings away, lock them up inside your heart and suffocate them. No more acting giddy or glowing, as Katie put it. That will betray you. Wear a mask if you don't know who you are anymore. Pretend to be Agnes if that's what it takes to get through this. Otherwise, the consequences will be dire. You risk losing it all.

Is this what madness is like—this back-and-forth debate in my head? A splash of cold water cools my hot eyes and quiets my nattering thoughts. I get busy with the day's chores to distract me, but as I'm tidying up the clutter, a folded piece of paper falls from my cloak. It is the sketch that Victor did. My portrait, in charcoal. This does not help me now. I should fling it into the fire, but I cannot bring myself to destroy it. The woman in the sketch has been rendered so tenderly. The face is comely, the expression almost noble if a little sad. The eyes hold some mystery there. Is this really how Victor sees me?

There is a ruckus at the door and now the cottage is overrun with children. I quickly fold the portrait and look for somewhere to hide it. A book will do. I slip the sketch into the musty pages of the Samuel Richardson novel, knowing Robert will never touch the thing. There is something strangely delightful and wicked about hiding such incriminating evidence inside a book titled Virtue Rewarded.

Grace is chasing her younger siblings, making them squeal like piglets, and now the goat is inside again. I watch them rampage, but do not scold or shush them. This is what is at stake. If Robert were to discover my infatuation, he would throw me out in an instant. He would exile me from the island itself, from my children, and that I could not bear.

A table is toppled, a dish breaks. The children freeze, holding their breath as they await a harsh rebuke from me.

"Take the rumpus outside," I say quietly. "And the goat, please. Off you go."

They stand shocked for a moment before wrangling the animal out the door.

Enough madness. I have to put a stop to this before it gets out of hand. Last night's meal sits cold in the pot. I portion some out into a bowl, along with a hunk of bread, and march my way up to Merryman croft. I don't bother to knock. Victor is busy with his work, hands deep inside some strange contraption. He is surprised, but happy to see me.

"Agnes! Come look what I have here. It is miraculous."

"No, thank you." My tone is flat, my face empty. I set the bowl and bread on the table. "Your meal."

"Oh. Thank you," he says. "A bit early, isn't it?"

"It's cold. You'll need to hang it over the fire if you want it warm."

He is confused by my coolness. "Is everything all right?"

I turn to go but stop at the door. "I won't be coming here anymore. I'll send Grace up with your meal from now on."

He extracts his hands from the infernal device and wipes them on a rag. "What? What have I done to offend you, Agnes? Please, tell me."

My hand goes up, stopping his approach. "I cannot be here. I'm sorry."

His expression moves from shock to hurt. "At least tell me why. I thought we were friends. You are, in fact, the only friend I have in the world right now."

"This has become something else. I have only myself to blame, but it is wrong, and it cannot go on." There is already a wobble in my voice, but I steel myself against it. Tears will only make this worse. "Goodbye, Victor. I wish you success with your work."

Quickstep out the door and down the path. I hear him calling after me, begging me to explain. I do not break stride, nor do I look back at the tenant of Merryman croft. This short, confusing chapter of my life is finished.

CHAPTER XXII

Jamie Grieve has been on my mind of late. I don't know why. It has been over thirteen years since I have seen him, and that last encounter was not a pleasant one for either of us. Was I cruel to him? When it was all said and done, I told myself that I was not being cruel to the boy, just honest. And yet, morsels of the past can get painted in ways that suit our favor, rather than the truth.

When I told Jamie that it was over, that I was going to wed Robert Tulloch of Eynhallow, the boy was crushed. He begged me to reconsider, arguing that a stranger, a man almost twice my age, could never make me happy. When I asked how he could possibly know this, Jamie told me that the man was simply in need of a wife, and not a true companion or lover. The widower Tulloch, he claimed, would never truly know me. Not the way he did. Open your eyes, he begged me.

Everyone was against Jamie. He was penniless and fatherless, they said. He had no prospects, and no future. They were all thrilled with the idea of wedding me off to Mr. Tulloch. Especially my stepmother, who all but pushed me out the door of my father's house. You'll not get another chance like this, she whispered to me. Take the widower's hand and do not let go.

All of this chatter was in my ears when Jamie tried to dissuade me. I put my foot down, incensed that Jamie would presume to know my heart better than I did. I told him my mind was made up, that my heart was closed to both him and our childhood dalliance. Was I cruel? At the time, I told myself I was simply being firm, but in hindsight, I believe I was cruel. Poor Jamie left in tears. That was when he made his vow to raise himself up in the world and prove himself worthy. That he would sail to the holy isle and save me from the trap I had walked into.

He never came, of course. I hope he is happy, wherever he is now. Did he meet some other girl and fall in love? I hope so. The lad had nothing, but he was a gentle soul. If I were to see Jamie again, I would beg his forgiveness for stomping his heart the way I did. But all of this is old history and dusty lore. Why does it come to mind now? Listen to me. As if I don't know the answer to that question. The tenant of Merryman croft has stirred those dead embers in my heart to life, and that absolutely terrifies me. When I told Victor I would no longer see him, the look in his eyes was not so different to what I saw in Jamie's all those years ago. Do I not know my own heart? Did I ever?

Every sound is flat, every color is gray. I go about my duties with all the enthusiasm of a slug. Robert is grating my nerves and the children seem overly boisterous. I keep reminding myself that I have done the right thing, but it rings hollow. If this is truly the right course of action, why do I feel so absolutely wretched? Thoughts can be such slippery eels. Mine slither back to the solitary man in the haunted cottage, alone and now friendless.

On the second day of my retreat, I send Grace out to bring the man his dinner. She makes no fuss this time as her opinion of the man has changed since the night he thawed out before our fire. Despite my resolve, I interrogate the poor girl when she returns from her task. How is the tenant? Is he happy? Busy at his work?

"He seems unwell," Grace tells me. "A bit pale and lifeless."

"How do you mean? Is he ill?"

Grace shrugs. "How should I know? He's rude, I can tell you that. When I brought his food, he hardly acknowledged me. He just sat in a chair and stared at the floor."

Without thinking, I pepper the girl with more questions. Did he eat? Did she ask him what the trouble was? Does the man need help?

My eldest daughter frowns at my pestering questions. "I have no idea. Nor do I care. The foreigner can fetch his own meals as far as I'm concerned."

"Grace, that's rude."

She grimaces at me. "Rude? He's the one who's rude. He barely acknowledged me. It's just as father says, these noble types are fatuous ninnies."

"All right, thank you, Grace."

The girl's eyes are sharp, scrutinizing me. "Why do you care?"

I tell her I don't and end the conversation. The evening passes as tortuously as the day. I stare at the timber beams all night, unable to sleep. Robert reaches for me in the dark. I push him away.

Another day unravels, as tedious and grating as the day before. My foul mood seems to infect the household as the children squabble endlessly, and Mr. Tulloch is impatient with us all. At one point, when Kit is being overly brash, he raises his hand to discipline the boy. I snatch his wrist, and whisper one word to him. "No."

He curses, gripes about what he's forced to endure, and stomps out of the cottage. Good riddance.

When the day winds down, I send Grace off with a meal for the Genevan. When she returns, I interrogate her as to the man's condition.

"Much worse," Grace replies. "He was haggard and out of sorts. There was a bruise on his cheek."

"A bruise? From what?"

"I asked, but he did not answer me," Grace says. "I don't want to go back there, mother. He scares me."

This comes as a surprise. "There's nothing to be afraid of, Grace. He's temperamental, that's all."

The girl doesn't believe me. "I think he's gone mad. He was muttering to himself and fiddling with a flintlock."

"The pistol?" I press her for details. According to Grace, the man seems deranged and focused solely on cleaning the weapon.

Where everything was gray to me, it now turns red. What on earth has come over Victor? And what does the bruise mean? His tormentor, the one Victor refuses to speak of. Has this fellow with the outlandish footprint assaulted Victor a second time? Is that why the flintlock was out? Does Victor mean to shoot his mysterious persecutor?

A cup slips from my hand as an even darker idea takes hold. Is the pistol meant for Victor himself? Does he plan to end his torment by taking his own life? His humors are so mercurial that I am afraid he just might commit such a rash act.

My earlier vow is shattered instantly as I tell Grace to mind the croft while I race up to the lonely cottage on the cliff. What have I done? Is it possible the man is heartbroken over my withdrawal or am I simply deluding myself? I do not know which way the compass points and every foolish decision I make is followed by another catastrophe.

The cottage is dark when I enter, and in even worse shambles than how I left it. I call his name but hear nothing save the wind at the shutter. The matches are scattered on the long table. I strike one to light the lamp.

The lonely tenant is sitting on the floor with his legs sprawled before him. The flintlock piece lays across his thigh. Am I too late? I see no blood.

"Victor, what are you doing?" I shake him like a drunk who needs rousing. "Look at me."

His eyes hold no kindness. "Have you come back to torment me? Like the fiend?"

"I was worried about you." I turn his face to the light. The flesh of his cheek is mottled dark. "Who did this to you? Was it the person you spoke of?"

"Go home, Agnes," he says. He pushes me away. "Go back to your loving children and your husband and your happy life. Do not torment me any further. Please."

He buries his face in his hands and openly weeps. The sight of it dumbfounds me. I have seen children weep, seen Katie rail in despair, but I have rarely witnessed a man cry thus. I don't know what to do. I am to the brim with pity and embarrassment at the same time.

"Stop it, Victor." I lift his chin to me. "Dry your eyes and man yourself. This is too much."

He drags a shirtsleeve across his eyes and shakes his head. "Forgive me."

I grant him a moment to compose himself. "Tell me what's happened? What is wrong?"

"Wrong?" he spews. "I am sick unto death of this wretched place. Of this work, of the obligation hanging over my head. And then you abandon me. You, my gentle and only friend on this godforsaken island, you have turned your back to me." He rises and staggers across the room. "Why have you come? To torment me further?"

The man is a wreck. But his pain is real enough, writ stark across his face. "It was not my intention to wound you, Victor. I am sorry."

"Then why deny me your company? You are the only good thing in my life now."

I fold my hands in my lap. "We mustn't talk of this."

"Why not? Why do you hide from me, Agnes?"

"Because I am afraid!" My outburst is like a cannonball, startling the man. I push him away. "I am afraid of what will happen. I cannot think clearly when I am around you. My head is fevered with a thousand impulses. My heart is ripped in two—one part with you, the other with my children."

Something different lights his eyes now. He takes a step forward. "Agnes, I didn't realize."

"Stop." My hand goes up to halt him. "Victor, I do not wish to be cruel, but I do not trust myself around you. Please. I have too much at stake to be made a fool of."

He stops. Runs a hand through the mop of hair. "I would not do that to you. I swear."

What a wretched mess this is. We remain on opposite sides of the room like opponents in a duel.

"I didn't know," he says. "I thought you were just humoring me. Being the good neighbor."

"Then you are an idiot."

He nods his head. "I am."

Neither of us knows what to say, so we remain silent and listen to the wind whistle under the door.

"This cursed place," he says, more to himself than to me. "I want nothing more than to leave it. To run away from all—"

His thought is clipped on the wing. Victor stands frozen, his eyes wide and staring. It is as if some unknown hand has stabbed him in the back.

"Victor? What is it? What's wrong?"

The fool rushes at me like a madman, sliding to his knees and almost bowling me over. "Run away with me, Agnes. We'll find a ship and leave this place forever."

"Have you lost your mind?" I twist out of his grip, but he won't let go. "I cannot run away with you."

"Yes, you can. I know you are unhappy here, too. You have confessed as much."

I tear his hands from my skirt. "I cannot abandon my children."

"We'll take them with us."

This is too much and too fast. I cannot think straight. "No, Victor. That is madness. I cannot."

He squeezes my arms. "Yes, you can. Don't you see? I can take care of you and your children. I have means. We'll go to the continent. I have a villa in Cologny. We can go there and be free, be shed of this place."

My heart vaults into my throat and I cannot breathe. I cannot think straight for the crash of thoughts churning through my mind. This is the stuff of faery tales and children's stories, not reality. It does not happen to plain, if overly tall, peasant women.

None of this is real. I am dreaming. I have fallen asleep at home and am dreaming all of it.

"Agnes," he says. "Kiss me."

I do as I'm told. And everything is terrifyingly, unnervingly real.

CHAPTER XXIII

Feral. That's the only word I can muster for my behavior. Something inside me snaps, a seal or a lock, and some other woman emerges. So bold, so angry, that I don't even recognize her. It should frighten me, but it does not.

Clothes are shed, torn, thrown off. I clutch the hair on the back of his head to expose his neck and all but bite into him. I go at him like a starving woman would run at a slab of beef. Who is this person? Agnes Eliza Tulloch is always the demure wife, accepting, granting, shushing to not wake the children.

Not this night. This night I am a berserker ravishing a milkmaid. It throws Victor for a spell. Like all men, he is used to being the one who dominates. It scares him a little. I can see it in his eyes, but it does not stop me. I am a boulder rolling downhill, gathering momentum. He winces at my bites. He tries to gain the upper hand and roll me under, but he is outmatched. I pin both of his wrists over his head and use him up.

He utters something in my ear, something about stopping before the inevitable, which is galloping close. I do not care in this moment. I couple him harder until I take what is mine. Out of breath, I collapse over him.

Sin.

The word pops to mind like a ruptured blister. I suppose it should mean something, but it does not. It is just a word, after all. One used like a cudgel to shame and control. In this moment, it has no more meaning to me than the word *dog* or *stone* or *salt*. Just words.

My hair, freed from its knot, splays all over him. Our slick flesh makes us slippery like eels. My voice cracks when I open my mouth.

"The children," I say. "You will shelter and love them?"

His eyes wheel about, trying to sharpen their focus. "What?"

"You will take care of my children? That's what you said."

"Yes. Yes, of course."

I press my lips against his neck. It is hot and salty. "Tell me about this place, Cologny. What is it like?"

He paints a picture of a paradise. A quaint manor overlooking a serene lake. Warm sunshine and the cool shade of sycamores. It sounds too good to be true. He carries on, becoming almost boastful, when his words are cut by an abrupt racket.

Fists, pounding on the door. We both spring out of bed. I am startled. Victor looks terrified.

"The fiend," Victor snarls. "Will he never leave me in peace?"

His tormentor, the giant with the prodigious footprint. Every shred of joy curdles into terror. This is followed by another jolt as a voice calls from outside. My child's voice.

"Is my mother there?" comes Grace's voice. "Sir, please open the door!"

Instinct preserves me as I shrink behind the screen. Shame crucifies me. The word *sin* grows teeth.

"A moment!" Victor cries out.

How I want to die, to crawl under a rock and hide my face. I hiss at Victor. "Do not tell her I am here. Tell her I've gone home."

Victor tugs on breeches and yanks the shirt over his head as he crosses to the door. I snatch up my discarded clothes, wondering what could possibly send Grace running here at this time of night. Disaster. One of the children is injured.

I hear the door scrape the floor, feel the wind blow into the cottage.

"Yes?" Victor says. "What is the matter, child?"

Grace's voice is frayed with panic. "I'm sorry, sir. Is my mother here? She is needed."

"She has gone home," Victor replies. "Did you not pass her on the way here?"

I hear Grace gasp and trip over her words. "No. Oh God. Where is she?"

"What is the problem? Is someone hurt?"

"Our neighbor has started her labors. Katie is screaming for mother's help."

A cold suspicion knocks me over. Did I cause this? Has my betrayal of the marital vows triggered my friend's overdue labor?

"Hurry back, child," Victor orders. "Your mother must have returned home by now."

"Thank you, sir."

I hear the door clatter home. I scramble into my clothes, cursing the stays that require so much tugging and lacing.

"Help me," I bark at him. He rushes to help cinch me back into order.

"Who is Katie?"

"My friend," I reply. "The one I told you about. Her babe is finally here."

"And you are the midwife?"

"Not a proper one," I tell him. "But there is no one else to fill the job."

I stomp into my boots and yank the man close for one last kiss before I bolt into the pitch and sprint across the heath. Every moment counts now, but I would be lying if I said I was not irked at the stubborn babe's timing.

The Kemp home is in chaos. Katie is squatting near the fire, held up by her fretting husband. All six children are backed against the wall, scared to death by their mother's awful keening.

"Why isn't she in bed?"

Tom is ashen. "She refuses to lie down!"

Poor Katie is all gnashing teeth and moans of torment. She grips my collar, clinging to me like a child waking from a nightmare. "Agnes, thank God. Something is wrong. Help me."

"You must get on the bed, Katherine. I cannot help until you lie down."

We get her situated on the bed and Katie's screams double in volume. Her husband holds her hand while I check the birthing canal. Open to four fingers. She is more than ready to push, but the baby will not come. This is the fifth time I have assisted Katie's labors. The previous four were championship efforts on my friend's part. Quick and with minimal fuss. Not this time. Her pain is out of control, and already there is too much blood on the sheets. As gently as possible, I probe to feel the baby's crown. What I find stops my heart. The hard lump of the head is not where it should be.

The husband's face turns another shade of pale when he sees my expression. "What is it? Agnes, what's wrong?"

Now I am afraid. I have never experienced a breech as a mother nor encountered it midwifing. An idea comes to me. Thank God my daughter is here now.

"Grace, run and fetch Victor," I say. "Tell him to hurry."

Tom is confused. "Who?"

"The tenant," I tell him. "He is a physician, of sorts. Go Grace. Hurry!"

I cannot let the babe come if it is rump first. I squeeze down on Katie's belly, kneading like a baker, to try and turn the infant from without. I have heard this is possible, but I have never seen anyone attempt it. Am I doing it correctly or am I hurting the little creature?

Katie is bellowing at me, calling me an oaf and a butcher. The pain is making her senseless. Tom holds her brow and coos to his wife to be calm. She bites at his hand. In the corner, the children are crying.

What is taking Victor so long? I need help. Just as I am cursing his name, the man charges through the door and takes in the bedlam. I bark at him to help me, whispering the problem into his ear.

He keeps his voice low but shakes his head. "I know nothing about birthing, Agnes."

"You must know something," I hiss. "The babe is wrong side up. If we cannot right it, it will come out blue. And Katie will be at risk."

Victor runs a hand through his hair. "Then we must cut it out."

"No!" My heart clamors in a panic. "It is too risky."

"There is no other way," he says. "The child will die unless we act."

I shake my head. "Katie will die if you cut her. Can you stitch her up properly? Can you promise that?"

Katie is raging and Tom begs us to do something. Time is running out. Victor whispers in my ear.

"It is the child or the mother," he says. "Surely, we must save the child?"

"No."

He does not agree. "But the child deserves a chance."

I snatch him by the collar. "Look there. Do you see those children? Six of them. They need their mother. We are not going to cut her."

Katie's face twists into a snarling mask. I beg her not to push, not yet. She screams at me to do something. The babe must come now. Then, with another ear-splitting bellow from the mother, the baby makes its appearance, haunches first. My heart stops, my hands freeze.

Pandemonium plays out. Katie's screams shake the timbers as she grits down, but the infant seems stuck. I reach in to tug and twist a leg out, terrified to exert too much force. Katie curses me again, bearing down hard, and then a tiny foot takes its first step into this world. I fear the babe will begin life with a broken leg. The other tiny leg slips through easily, thank Christ. The sheer amount of blood is frightening me, but there is no time to fret as the child keeps coming. It stops and my greatest fear plays out. The head is stuck. I cannot get a good grip on the slippery thing, and I do not like the way the cord is tangled. If it doesn't happen now, we will lose the little creature.

Tom is hollering like a lunatic and the children are scared to death at hearing their mother's agony. Grace is sobbing, unable to help. Victor shoulders me aside and takes over.

"A little force now," he grumbles. "Then we'll have it. Here we go."

The sound of my friend's agony is unbearable. The babe is trapped at the neck and will come no further. Victor falters, becomes desperate. He looks at me with an ashen face, then lowers his head in defeat. I push him aside and take over, but there is no firm grasp on the slippery body. Katie howls for mercy, but I beg her to push again. This goes on forever. Everyone in the room is screaming now and my ears split and suddenly the babe is free, slipping into my hands like an eel. It does not look right, too blue by far. Victor severs the cord and I try to rub it to life, but it does not stir. I scoop fluid from its tiny mouth and slap the infant's back to clear the airways, but no cry issues from the fragile thing. Katie collapses and Tom is already asking whether it is a boy or a girl. I cannot look at him right now, let alone tell him that his question is pointless. I swaddle the babe and hand it to Victor because Katie is stirring again. She is beyond exhausted, but the afterbirth must come. It slips out with another push and Grace comes to take it away.

The babe is now in the arms of its father and the father is surrounded by its siblings. All are in tears as they say both hello and goodbye. The vignette rips my heart, but I cannot stop to mourn. The blood will not staunch. It keeps coming, pooling on the bed and cascading to the floor. Katie is terrifyingly pale, whiter than the sheet under her.

Victor is at a loss. Why did I think he could help? I bark at Grace to find Tom's whiskey and soak a linen with it. The only remedy I know is to pack the canal to stop the blood. The whiskey may burn the bleeding vessels closed. All that is left is to pray.

Will the Almighty hear our tiny prayers? Surely, he must have heard Katie's howls of torment? The citizens of Aberdeen would have heard those cries. It is pointless to speculate, I suppose. Katie grows weaker by the minute, and no amount of prayer will revive her.

She is gone before the sun rises.

CHAPTER XXIV

There is nothing more to be done. I clean up and make my friend as presentable as possible, but there is simply no way to make the deceased look like they are resting. Death is a promise that cannot be made pretty. I want to nestle the swaddled babe in the crook of Katie's arm, but her husband will not part with it yet. He rocks it before the fire as if hoping to warm the child. I shepherd Victor and my daughter out the door. No one says goodbye.

The sun is up, and the wind is gentle. It is a beautiful day. Grace will not let go of my hand. I should not have brought her. Why do I lean on her so much? The girl is only twelve. Far too young to have witnessed such a tragedy.

The three of us are at a loss for words, but oddly, we are all reluctant to part. Gulls call out overhead.

"I am terribly sorry for your loss," Victor says.

My head shakes in disbelief. "Poor Katie. It doesn't seem real."

Grace begins to cry. Victor clears his throat, unsure of how to console her. He bows and says good day to us, before marching uphill to his cottage.

We arrive home to a cold hearth and sleeping children. Mr. Tulloch dozes in his chair. I touch his shoulder to rouse him and give the terrible news. He makes the sign of the cross.

I start the fire, but I am too tired to do anything else. There is a duty to be performed, but I am dreading it. Mr. Tulloch goes out to relay the sad news to the other households on the island. He and George Heddle meet to hammer together a coffin. Mr. Dearness joins them, bringing along all the spare timber he has. When the children wake, I tell them as gently as possible what has happened. Our little cottage becomes a very sad place this day. I worry about Grace. She is unusually quiet after what she has seen. Will it haunt her dreams? How could it not?

I don't know how much time passes, but soon there is the knock that I am dreading. I open the door to find Nelly Heddle and Mary Dearness calling. Both are wearing heavy aprons, their arms bound in black crepe.

"Good morning, Agnes," Mary says very softly. "We should get started."

Nelly, ever the flinty one, is not so soft. She looks me up and down with something close to disdain. "Have you not even changed?"

I look down to see the crust of blood and gore drying on my skirts. Oh God.

"Hurry along, Agnes," Nelly says. "Before the day slips away from us."

Letting Nelly Heddle into my home is something I prefer not to do. She always sneers and holds her nose, but I have no choice at the moment. They wait while I hurriedly wash the blood from my hands and change my clothes. I pin back my hair without looking into the mirror, and the three of us head out.

"Isn't Grace coming with us?" asks Mary. "Surely she is old enough to help now."

I march without looking at her. "She's seen enough."

Nelly clearly disagrees, even though her pinched mouth stays shut. We walk.

Mary touches my elbow. "What happened?"

I relate the events as best as I can. The women listen and shake their heads at the tragedy of it. Mary asks God to preserve the souls of Katie and her child.

A gentle knock on the Kemp door. Will lets us in, still puffy and red-eyed from sobbing. I whisper to him that it will be best if he takes his siblings to my house. Grace will make them breakfast. He shepherds the slow children out the door. Tom is still pacing before the fire, rocking the babe as if trying to get it to sleep.

Mary goes to him. It's for the best as I do not think Tom wants to look at me right now. Mrs. Dearness is gentle with the bereaved man, telling him that he has done well keeping the babe safe, but now there are duties to be performed. The last thing he wants to do is let the babe go, but Mary persists gently. He lets her take the child, reminding her to support the darling little head. It takes all I have to keep from bursting into tears all over again. All three of us breathe a little relief when he kisses his wife's brow and steps outside.

I am not up to this task, but there is no choice in the matter. We get to work. Water is heated for both the wash basin and the scrub tub. We roll the body one way and then the other to strip the bed. I wonder idly who had the forethought to lay the canvas down to protect the mattress of husk and straw, Katie or Tom?

Nelly takes the sheets to the washtub while Mary and I tug the shift from our friend. She is already cool to the touch and her eyes have taken on the glassy sheen that tells of a departed soul. We sop up the dried blood with warm water and wash cloths. A fresh basin of water is prepared, and we bathe her from crown to toe. All three of us take a break from the toil to look over Katie's clothes and decide what she should be buried in. A dress is chosen, but no shoes. Getting our friend into her funeral clothes takes another hour of tugging and straining. Mary lets slip a naughty word and we all laugh. It is strange how something silly can break the heaviness in the air. I suppose we all needed it. Even Nelly, the prude, laughs.

With that task accomplished, an even grimmer one awaits, but we all dither and procrastinate. No one has the stomach for it. Regarding the tired faces of my companions, I volunteer to perform the task and shoo them on home.

Mary frets, reluctant to leave. "Are you sure, Agnes? Maybe we should do it together?"

Nelly despises this idea, but, to her credit, she says nothing. I tell them it is fine. Katie was my friend, and it seems only right.

"I suppose she would want it that way," agrees Mary.

Both women kiss Katie's brow before they leave. And now I am alone. On the table rests the swaddled bundle. Did the parents have a name picked out? I should know, but for the life of me, I do not remember. I remove the swaddling to soak in the wash tub and warm some more water for the basin. The baby seems so tiny compared to the bulge of Katie's belly. And so very, very fragile. It is a wonder any child survives at all. The little thing conjures memories of my own lost babes, but those will only make this worse, so I push them aside and get busy. I wash and pat the child dry, and then swaddle it in clean linen. A gentle kiss to its frowning little face.

"Back to Heaven you go," I whisper.

I lift the bundle and nestle it into the crook of its mother's arm. Outside, I can hear the hammer and the saws at work. Soon, the men will enter with the narrow coffin, and we will place my friend into it. With that accomplished, I can return home where I can fall to pieces in private.

"Goodnight, sweet Katie," I tell my friend before I leave. "You were loved, and you will be missed."

CHAPTER XXV

Nary a cloud in sight as grief settles over our little community. We are so few in number that the loss is felt in every home. It is a peculiar thing—everyone wants to help, but there is nothing to be done. Who can alleviate the family's pain? Only the Almighty can, but that doesn't stop us from trying, of course. I prepare a dish and bring it to the Kemp family, as do Mary and Nelly. There is plenty of food should any of the mourners get hungry, but no one has much of an appetite. All this food, and barely anything is touched. The Kemp children sit like mutes, unwilling to speak to anyone. Tom assures us that he is fine, but his words trail off or he loses his thoughts in a kind of haze. Propped up by a makeshift bier near the window is the coffin holding mother and child. Three days of visitation, concluding with the funeral.

I stay busy looking after the Kemp family as best I can, seeing to the tasks that fall under a mother's purview. This is partly out of need, but, if I am honest with myself, it is more about running from the pain. If I stop, then the full weight of Katie's passing will catch me up and knock me down. How am I going to endure without her prickly wit or sympathetic ear? Even at the worst of times, Katie could find a way to twist any situation bearable. Or at least let us laugh at its absurdity. How am I supposed to carry on without her?

All of this is further complicated by the incident that preceded Katie's labor. I am still shocked by my actions. I am not some wanton coquette, and yet, I did what I did. And the cascade of events—to go from ardent coupling to the frenzy of childbirth to the sum of mortality. My God. Even now, there is an eerie suspicion that these events are linked—that my indiscretion had somehow triggered my friend's demise. I sinned, but she paid the price. I know that is preposterous, but it still gnaws at my insides like a pestilent infection.

I avoid the tenant all the while. It is simply too much to bear. I can manage the moment at hand, no more and no less.

My own little world is much subdued. The children are quiet in their sadness. Kit and Meg are not fighting and that in itself is a relief. Effie is too young to understand, but she feels the temperature in the room and keeps her voice to a whisper. Grace is the one who worries me. The girl tells me she is fine, but she is not. It is there in the way she sweeps crumbs from the table or scolds the goat to get out of her way. She goes about her chores with a clipped manner that makes me think she too is running from something she doesn't want to contemplate.

I find a quiet moment to speak to her as we salt scrub the table. I chew my lip over how to broach the topic. She can be skittish, our Grace. Open with the wrong word and the child may simply shut down like an irked clam.

"You must be tired, sweetheart," I mention to her, scouring the wood with the brush. "I heard you get up in the night. Did you have trouble sleeping?"

Grace sprinkles more salt on the table. "It was nothing."

In truth, I did not hear her get up out of bed. I heard her sobbing into her pillow. Maybe the direct approach is best after all. I touch her elbow to make her look at me.

"I am sorry you had to see such an awful thing," I tell her. "I appreciated your help, but if I had known how it would play out, I never would have asked you to come."

She stops scouring. "I can't stop seeing it. Or hearing it. How poor Katie screamed like that. Jesus save us."

I fail to say anything that might make sense or mitigate her pain.

The girl grinds the brush again, working along the grain like I've taught her. "Is it always like that? So horrific and terrifying?"

"It is difficult, but not always so harrowing. You were there when Mary Elizabeth was born." Katie's youngest. Grace was ten at the time. I brought her along to observe, to break her in slowly before beginning her apprenticeship into midwifery. Little Grace was shocked by the birth, but the horror of it was wiped clean by the fascination of a newborn.

"It is a dangerous thing," I tell her. "Every mother straddles the razor when they ferry a new soul into the world. But Death is a stingy thing, jealous of every sprout of life. It sidles close in birthing, eager to swallow both mother and child in its pettiness."

Although I try, I am not always the best teacher. The grimace on my daughter's face is evidence of that. Instead of educating the girl, I have nauseated her. I have tried exactly one time to explain to Grace, in very basic terms, how babies are conceived. The girl turned green at the thought.

Grace flaps the whole thing away with a hand. "I never want to be a mother if that's the case. I'd sooner die alone."

I suppose I should try to dissuade this notion, but I do not. The day winds down like any other, save for this pall that settles like dust over everything. After dinner, Grace asks if I am taking the stranger his meal, but I am not. I do not think about the man or what transpired, and I continue to not think of it long into the night as my husband and children snore around me.

Up and about this morning, on very little sleep. Small faces are scrubbed, and hair is combed, plaited. Everyone struggles into their church clothes, which are nothing fancy and little more than our plain clothes with all the buttons done up. Black crepe, saved from the last funeral, binds every arm. Effie is not doing well, another chill and runny nose, but she is obedient and eager to please her mam. We file out the door and join the other islanders at the Kemp farm.

Dickie, the Eynhallow horse, is fitted into the wagon trace, flicking its tail as the men bring out the coffin. The Kemp family step out into the sunlight and follow the funereal wain. Simon and Mary Elizabeth are in tears, but their older siblings bear only blank expressions. Too numb to weep. That's the funny thing with tears. Despite the common phrase of crying one's eyes out, there are always more where they came from.

A somber procession to the little graveyard near the kirk ruins. The headstones tilt this way and lean that way, battered by the wind and rain. There are two small markers that bear the name Tulloch. One belongs to Mr. Tulloch's first wife, Marie, who passed before the age of thirty. I do not remember what she died of. The other is a simple wooden block that marks the resting place of my babes who did not survive. Two names are chiseled into the wood here. One is *Robert*, named after his father, and the other reads *Agnes*. We had not settled on a name before the baby girl passed, and Mr. Tulloch thought it clever to give her my name. It is a tad unsettling to see both of our names here, as if the graves are waiting for us.

The funeral service is short but adequate. The Kemp family watch the casket being lowered into the ground and my heart bottoms out for them anew. How will they carry on without the thumping, raucous heart of the family?

As Mr. Dearness says a final prayer over the grave, I hear someone hiss. Nelly, to my left, spying something in the distance.

"Imagine showing his face here," she grouses to her husband. "The nerve."

I turn to see a solitary figure on the heath, watching from afar. Monsieur Frankenstein keeps a respectful distance, hat in hand. Is Nelly unaware that he tried to help Katie? Or does she blame the man for her death?

The service comes to an end and the Kemp clan walk away in silence. Everyone follows, save for George Heddle, who has volunteered to backfill the grave and tamp it flat with his spade. As we make our way back across the island, I see George catch up to join his wife. Confused, I turn to look back at the graveyard.

The solitary figure stands alone at the graveside with his jacket removed and shirtsleeves rolled up. He plunges the shovel into the dirt and throws it into the narrow grave.

CHAPTER XXVI

The reception is held at the Kemp home. We may be solemn and respectful at the passing of our fellows, but we are also a people who express mourning with celebration. It is a chance to tweak Death's nose and spit in its face as we remember our dead. Mr. Tulloch has uncorked one of his finer bottles and keeps the men's glasses steady. The women are allowed one miserly dram. When I pour a second, Robert scowls at me, but I ignore him. There will be hell to pay for this later, but I do not care. I care about so few things nowadays, it seems.

We eat, we drink, and we mourn. Someone brings out a fiddle, but the sound of it only makes us sadder, so the instrument is put away.

Late into the afternoon, the door opens, and every head turns to see the stranger. Silence follows. My stomach lurches so hard I fear I am going to be sick. Someone clucks their teeth at the man's cheek for showing his face. Victor Frankenstein nods at all assembled before crossing the room to shake the widower's hand and offer his condolences. Mr. Tulloch's lips have been loosened with drink, and he stands to inform the stranger that this is a private affair. Islanders only if you please. Victor nods and prepares to leave.

My blood is up by the slight. Is grief something to be selfish about? My own lips are a little loose, it seems. I object, loudly.

"The gentleman tried to help," I inform my husband. I hear Nelly gasp at my impudence, but I roll it along. "Let the man stay."

George tuts that it's not right, but Tom overrules him. "It's true," says the bereft father. "He did his best to save my Katie, as did Agnes. Please, stay, sir. You are welcome."

The matter is settled. Mr. Dearness gets the stranger a glass, eager to engage the man on spiritual matters. I suppose he sees an opportunity to redeem the heathen's soul. I am grateful for Tom's intervention here. His words may well mitigate the punishment I receive later tonight for my sedition. Mr. Tulloch is eyeing me with a chilling regard.

The afternoon limps into evening. The children become restless. Daisy the goat brays outside the window, wanting to come in. The man from Geneva stands huddled with the other fellows around the hearth. He seems to have been accepted by the Orkneymen. Victor risks a glance or two in my direction. Some time later, I am at a side table, picking over the platters although I am not hungry. Victor appears at my side, spooning a dollop of salted herring onto his plate. My hands go cold as I glance over my shoulder, but no one seems to notice us.

"I need to speak with you," he whispers.

"Not here," I say quietly.

"Then when?"

"Tomorrow," I reply. "I'll bring your supper as usual. I don't think you should linger here too long."

Moving quickly, I put the distance of the room between us. Did we make a display of ourselves? Do my cheeks bloom red in shame? My fears are for naught. The assembled mourners are too far into their tipple to notice anything. Even the normally pinched-faced Nelly Heddle is getting sloppy with her words. Mr. Dearness, emboldened with spirits, seems determined to engage the foreigner in matters ecclesiastical, causing our visitor to look for an escape. Victor offers his condolences once again to Tom, bows to the others, and leaves. My relief is like water tossed onto a fire, and I sink into a chair.

The night carries on, and the children become tired, irritable. Effie is already curled into my lap, snoozing like a cat. Time for bed. The children's father is by the hearth, palavering loudly with the other men. Would he even notice that I'd gone? Before I can get to my feet, Thomas Kemp rises before the fire and rattles his cup on the mantle to draw everyone's attention.

"Friends," says the widower. "I want to thank you all for your kindness today. I know my Katie would be much pleased to see how the peoples of this island protect and shelter one of their own in difficult moments. When sorrow breaks on our shores, the good people of Eynhallow come together. To you, good ladies and gentlemen."

A mumbled hurrah goes up. Tom has always been liked by everyone on the island. A good man with an honest heart. He has never borne the condescension of people who think you beneath them even when you tower a head above them. Even if he had, I doubt Tom would hold a grudge. He is not petty. My own pettiness grows a sharp edge to it after too many drams, it seems. Wait, his toast is not over.

"I know Katie would hate to miss this gathering, because she loved nothing more than to raise a glass. I used to ask her how she always found the positive side of things, and she'd say that life was too short, and there's time enough for misery in the grave. Hold onto the sun while it's shining, she'd say, because our time to kick a jig is too quick by far!"

Laughter rings out and glasses are raised in honor of our departed girl. Despite his bravado, poor Tom is again in tears as he tries to wrap his eulogy in a tidy bow. He fails. He speaks directly to his dead wife, declaring his love and despairing how his family will carry on without her. He falters and Mr. Heddle fails to catch him before he collapses. The islanders are on their feet, fetching water and fanning the man's face.

A general melee ensues. I tug Mr. Tulloch aside and tell him that I'm taking the children home.

"Now?" he sputters. "At this crisis?"

"There is nothing I can do to alleviate the man's pain. The children are tired."

He yanks his arm from my grip as a wash of sour contempt colors his features. My patience with his moods ran thin long ago, so I gather the children and herd them home. Effie remains asleep in my arms the whole way, and I put her to bed as she is. The other three I help change into their nightshirts and tuck into bed. I sit by the fire for a while, chewing on Tom's words about life being too short. Katie's words, actually. How did she put it? Our time to kick a jig is short.

There is irony in this and, as stupefied as I may be with drink, it does not escape me. I sit here in this cramped cottage, stewing over her words while my thoughts keep running off to the stranger uphill and his declarations made in a feverish moment. How he asked me to run away with him, how he promised to take me and my children far away from this holy isle.

The hour grows even later, and I am still stewing. When the door bangs open, I realize my mistake. I should have gone to bed long before the lord of the manor returned home. He is beyond drunk and wallowed in a grim mood. He tells me I have disgraced him this night by going against him and defending that lecher in the Merryman cottage. Judas, he calls me, for not bolstering his side of the disagreement. On and on he rants, working himself into a lather until finally he raises his hand to strike me.

One lash, which I accept. But I am nothing like our Savior who endured thirty-three of them. When he raises his hand a second time, I snatch him by the collar and jerk him clean off his feet. His head smacks hard against the stone wall. He tries to break free, but forgets that my strength dwarfs his the same way my height does. Vexed, he spits on me. My sight blows red. I smack his skull against the stone one more time and I hurl him across the room. He crumples to the ground like a sack of blighted potatoes. I back away, mortified by my sudden taste for violence.

The light from the embers in the hearth is low, but it is not dim enough to hide the whited eyes of my children. All of them, Effie included, gape in horror after witnessing their father beaten senseless. My youngest weeps. Grace claps a hand over Effie's mouth to silence her.

Scalded raw by the shame, I fling the pitcher of water over the embers to make everything dark.

CHAPTER XXVII

The urge to deny ugly truths is on full display this morning. I make no mention of last night's violence and Mr. Tulloch claims to not remember a thing. He makes a limp joke about overindulging and waking up on the floor. The children do not speak a word, eating their gruel quickly and rushing outside. The millstone grinds on. How eager we all are to sweep the nastiness under the rug and carry on.

Katie's passing is still so raw that I decide to visit her today. I pluck a few strands of coltsfoot and sea thrift on the way to lay on her grave. The wind is in a mood, blowing at my back before turning about-face to buffet me sideways. It rips the petals from my flowers leaving me with only green stalks in hand. Even this I cannot do right, it seems. I let the wind have the stalks too.

Stepping through the willowy grass of our churchyard, I find my friend's resting place in a terrible state. The earth has been haphazardly backfilled and not tamped flat as should be. It is not even properly filled, leaving an oblong crater in the earth. The wooden marker that bears the name Katherine Jane Kemp leans askew as if it has been tampered with. It is disgraceful, to say nothing of disrespectful. When Victor offered to alleviate George of this labor yesterday, I thought it such a kind gesture. I do not think that anymore seeing the poor job he's done of it. I can only guess that Victor, being from the aristocratic class, hasn't had much truck with the use of a spade. Why volunteer to do a job if you can't do it right?

Since I have no flowers for a tribute, the least I can do is correct Victor's shoddy workmanship here. There are no tools about, so I simply use my hands to claw the loose soil back over the grave. When the soil is leveled, I tamp it flat with my hands. It would be easier to do this with my feet, but then I would literally be dancing on my friend's grave. How Katie would have a good laugh at that.

Something is amiss. A tingling on the back of my neck relays the uneasy feeling of being watched. I scan my position but see nothing out of the ordinary. The heath, the sea, the ruins of the kirk. No leering Thomas or nosy Nellies. Is it just this location? The churchyard has never bothered me before, but perhaps that's changed now that my friend is interred here.

Kneeling before the stone, I brush the soil from my darkened palms and pour out my heart to my friend. Katie was always such a good listener. Why should death change that? I tell her the whole tawdry story of my flirtations with the stranger, culminating in the shattering of vows and a tumble in the straw. I cry, I vent, confessing it all. I wonder if Katie is giggling in her coffin, having a good laugh at my ridiculous predicament. I am grateful that the wind is louder than my words. I would not want it to carry my confession to eager ears over the heath. Can you imagine?

When I conclude my sordid tale, I feel absolutely drained but my heart is not half so heavy as before. Katie, ever the good listener, has lent me her ear and helped in the way she always knew best.

Brushing the grass from my knees, I thank her for her kindness. "I'll come visit again soon, my friend. Rest now."

There it is again! That creeping sensation of being watched. Still, I see no one observing from a distance. Grief must be scrambling my brains. Who would spy on me? I am not that interesting a person. Shrugging it off, I turn to make my way up the path when something rustles in my periphery. God help me, I see it.

A thing, for I know not what else to call it, emerges from the sandstone ruins. A figure of such enormous stature that it bends under the archway before it can stand at its full, ungodly height. Is it a daemon of the pit or one of the trolls of legend that haunt this isle? My mind all but shuts down trying to understand this creature of gray flesh and strange proportions. The wind whips its dark hair around a lurid face.

It blocks my path.

The scream echoing in me will not come out. My legs will not run, stricken fast with terror at this hideous thing.

"Hold."

It speaks. A voice of ruination, an echo from a tomb. "Do not run," it says.

"Stay away!" My own voice is high and trembling. "Do not hurt me."

"Do as I say, and I will leave you unmolested," it says. "Do you understand?"

Too petrified to speak, all I can do is watch it take another stride toward me. That face. The pallid flesh is taut over bone, revealing the structure of skull and sinew beneath. The eyes watery and half-lidded. Without life almost, and yet the thing moves and communicates. Here stands the apparition I saw on the shore, the same as Katie witnessed on the heath.

I cannot look at it. I plead with it to leave me alone.

"Disturb the man no more," it says. "Stay away from him. You must do this."

"Who?"

It shambles closer, towering over me. My God, it must be eight feet tall.

"I have watched you dally with the man," says the thing. "No more. You must not distract him from his work."

My blood can run no colder. It means Victor. It has seen us, spied on us. Oh God.

"Who are you?"

The creature, for I cannot call it a man, does not reply. Its gruesome eyes glare down at me through the stringy black hair. Somewhere, I muster the courage to challenge the thing.

"You are Victor's tormentor. The one who has hounded him and made his life miserable."

"I am."

My eyes dart around, desperate for help, but all I see is the plain of rolling grasses. No saviors, no help anywhere.

"Why can't you leave him alone? Why must you torment him so?"

"He has transgressed against me," the thing says. "He will make it right or I will torment him to his deathbed."

What diabolical bond is tethered between Victor and this monstrous figure? Did the Genevese summon this fiend from the pits of Hell?

My voice quavers like that of a frightened child. "What are you?"

The creature's eyes roll down my frame and up again to my eyes. "His son."

"Lies. Victor has no son or family. He is not wed."

"His words?" the thing says. "Which you accepted without question? The man is a liar and a miscreant." Its massive hand rises, gray flesh and blackened nails, and pounds its breast. "Here is his son, his issue. He denies it but sire me he did."

Lies. The creature before me is not even human. No man fathered it, no mother gave birth to it.

"Am I to take your word as truth? Victor is a good man, where you are a fiend. You spit lies and stink of the grave. Leave me be."

"He has bewitched you," it says. "Open your eyes, woman. See the man for what he is, not what you wish to see."

"More lies." I cinch my shawl tighter as if to protect me. A suit of armor would not shield me from this towering obscenity. "Let me pass."

Again, the thing blocks my escape. "I have watched you," it says. "Not just with Frankenstein. I've observed you at home. You have a mate and children. You are blessed by the core of happiness that is family. Why do you dally with the stranger? Why court disaster thus?"

I have no choice but to look away. Not content with terrifying me, the fiend wishes to mortify me with his questions. I refuse to dignify them with a response.

Another step forward. His musk is overbearing. It is like wild game but cut with the smell of the charnel house. He continues to torment me.

"Are you so unhappy, that you would risk everything you possess for a dalliance? I do not understand. Explain this to me."

"Get away from me!" I retreat one more step. "I do not answer to you. Who are you to question me? To spy on me?"

"Do you think he will save you? He breaks vows as easily as he makes them. Know that. Walk away, woman. Before he ruins you."

My blood heats up, takes hold of my tongue. "Do not moralize to me, you freak. Get away from me."

The creature is swift, and his hand is cold. It wraps all the way around my throat. Gently, but with the promise of a snap.

"Heed me. Stay away and distract him no further. His work is almost complete. Once he has given what is promised, you can ruin your life with him to your heart's content. Until then, stay away."

As strong as my hands are, they cannot tear his grip from my throat nor the thumb on my windpipe. When he releases me, I collapse to the clover gasping for air. The world spins sickeningly. When I finally catch my breath, I am alone on the empty heath. The creature is gone.

CHAPTER XXVIII

The children are outside when I return home, breathless from the run. They complain when I shoo them inside and slam the door closed. There is no brace to secure it, so I drag the heavy seaman's chest over to block it. Daisy bleats outside the window and Meg is relentless in her pleas to bring her pet inside. I capitulate and secure the door once the goat is safe. Confused, the children protest until I make up some nonsense about a coming storm. Grace is not so easily fooled, however. She pulls me aside and keeps her voice down.

"What is it? You look like you've seen a ghost."

I squeeze her hand. "There is something on the island with us. Something dangerous."

Her eyes widen. "What is it? Should we not tell Father?"

Damn my clumsy tongue. I explain that I have told her father, but the man does not believe me. For now, we will stay inside until the danger has passed. When she asks again what the thing is, I tell her I am not sure. A giant? A troll? The girl's eyes waver between fright and the uncomfortable suspicion that her mother is unwell. I should not have said anything, but my nerves are still raw with panic.

What to do now? Do I run to Victor to see if he is safe? I have a hundred questions about the thing that accosted me, but I am wary of the brute's warning to stay away. My patience is low. When Daisy bumps me from behind, I warn Meg to control her pet, or I will roast it over a spit.

By late afternoon, a plan emerges as I cook a vat of pottage. When it is ready, I wrap a cloth over the hot handle and march the children outside. The sky to the east is painting the clouds red, which bodes of a coming storm. Very well, bring it on. A knock at the door of the Kemp home and young Will lets us in. Tom seems genuinely pleased to see me and the children. The monotony of grief has worn the poor man down and he's in want of distraction. Happier still to be fed as I hang the vat over his fire. We chat for a bit. The children are doing as well as can be expected and Tom himself just shrugs and says he carries on. What else is there to do?

"Are you all right, Agnes?" he asks. "You look a little peaked."

My hands are restless birds that will not settle. "Just a little tired. Are you hungry?"

"Not really," he says. "But the children must be. I can't remember if I fed them today."

Grace helps me dole out the stew and the racket inside the cottage stills as everyone eats. I ladle one more bowl and tell Tom that I'm going to run this up to the tenant on the north end. I doubt that man has eaten either.

The march up to Merryman croft is fraught as I keep glancing behind me for any sign of the giant. The call of a gull startles me to quicken my pace until I reach the cottage. I enter without knocking. No fire, no candles, no Victor. Why isn't he here? Calling out, I check the room scribbled in symbols only to find it vacant. That leaves the second room, the one Victor asked me to stay out of. I do not have time to dither over a promise, but just as I am about to push it open, the door reels back and the man from Geneva steps through.

"Agnes?" He closes the door quickly and rushes to me, arms open. "Thank God, you've come."

I stop him in his tracks. Victor is clad in a leather apron that is red with blood and speckled with bits of hair and flesh.

"Good Lord, Victor. What on earth is all over you? Why is there blood?"

Thrown off stride, he seems almost surprised at the gore on his apron. "Oh dear, what a mess. An animal. Part of my work, you see."

"What animal?"

"A seal. I poached one from the shore."

"Take it off, please," I say.

He tosses it aside and takes hold of my arms. "Kiss me," he says.

I do as he asks, but my rattled nerves ruin the moment.

He leans back, confused. "What is wrong? You're shaking."

"I was accosted today. With violence."

His anger is immediate. "Mr. Tulloch?"

I shake my head and back away. "Your tormentor. He followed me to the graveyard."

The color leeches from his face. "My God. He showed himself to you?"

"Victor, what is he? Is he a man? He seems more troll than human."

"Did he hurt you?" His eyes go to my neck. Turning my chin to one side, he inspects the bruises on my throat. "He did this to you?"

"How do you know this fiend? Where did he come from?"

Shame colors his cheeks now. He hangs his head and runs a hand through his hair. "I am sorry, Agnes. I warned him to stay away from you."

Anger in my belly now, sour and hot. "Warned him? How does that thing know about us? Does it know what transpired?"

"No, no," he assures me. "He's seen you come and go, that is all."

I meet his gaze. "He claimed to be your son. Is that true? How is that even possible? The man is a giant."

"Lies," Victor tells me. "His mind is unwell and feverish. He deludes himself into thinking we are kin. There is no blood between us, I assure you."

"And yet he has some power over you. How? What possible hold could this wretch have over you?"

"The ultimate hold," Victor says. "Life and death. Happiness. Maybe my soul, in the end."

My wick is short this day. "Stop speaking to me in riddles and tell me what claim he has over you."

"I cannot!" He backs away from me, his features an anguished grimace. "One day I will untangle this unholy mess, but not now. Not this night."

The man's breathing turns to gasps and he sobs. My anger ebbs and pity floods in. I hold the man. "Surely, it cannot be so hopeless. Help me understand."

His grip tightens on my arm. "I cannot. I just want him to leave me in peace."

He is like a man drowning in his own grief, but I do not know how to save him. "How long will this go on?"

His temperament takes another wild turn. Eyes bright and eager as they seek mine. "Soon! I am almost finished my work. My obligation. Don't you see, Agnes? I am almost free."

Hopeful news, but now is the topic I have feared to broach. Impulsive words spoken hot in the untidy stew of passion. "And what then? What of us? Do you still want to run away with me?"

His hands clasp my head, pulling me close. "Yes! My obligation will be fulfilled by the midnight hour. Then we will be free. I have procured a boat, ready to leave at a moment's notice. We will flee this cursed isle and never look back. Go home. Pack."

My voice is cool and sober. "And the children? You said you would take care of us all."

"God, yes!" He pulls me close and spins round the cramped cottage. "Bring the children. Pack their things tonight and be ready. I will collect you at dawn."

"Tell me you're serious." I halt our dance and pin his arms to his sides. There can be no equivocation on this matter. "I will not put the children at risk. Tell me you mean this with your whole heart."

"Pack and be ready to go by first light. Tonight, I fulfill my end of a devilish bargain. Tomorrow, we will row away from this place and never look back." He waltzes me to the door. "But until then, I must not be disturbed, understand? Promise me."

I promise to wait for him, and we depart after a hurried, clumsy kiss. Rain sweeps in as he opens the door and I charge out, draping my shawl over my head. The storm has hit with an almost biblical vengeance, soaking me to the bone, but I barely feel its clammy chill. My heart is turning too many flips to feel the cold raindrops.

I am leaving this place. I am rescuing my children from a dreadful upbringing. It is almost too good to be true.

CHAPTER XXIX

The light from the hearth unfolds over a depiction of domestic bliss. The children sit chatting quietly or playing a game. It seems a shame to break it up. Tom has a good laugh as I drip rainwater all over his floor. Drying my face, I consider asking if the children could spend the night here. There is going to be a titanic row when Mr. Tulloch finds me packing and I would prefer the children not see such a thing. There will be hot words and cold fists. But I cannot ask that of the widower. His cottage is small, with barely enough room for the six children he has. How can I ask him to shelter four more?

The children grouse like old men when I tell them it is time to go. Effie lifts her arms, wanting to be carried and I cannot say no to the girl. I thank Tom for the hundredth time, gather the children and we bolt into the rain, screeching all the way home. Thankfully, the house is empty. I tell the children to get ready for bed and hang their wet clothes before the fire.

The chest at the foot of my bed is not large, but it is sturdy and will hold what we need, because we do not possess much. I unpack the linen and finer clothing from the chest, putting the stuff aside. At the bottom of the cedar lined casket lies a simple wool gown of blue with green piping. It is the dress I was married in, and saved now only for formal occasions. Will it be fancy enough for my new life with Victor, or will it seem drab in comparison to his usual class of delicate lords and ladies? The dress seems to mock me now, with worm holes in the wool and mouse droppings in the lace. The dismal thing is returned to the chest and buried under my other plain garments and the children's meager clothes. The compartment is not even half full.

What else to take? We are starting a new life, but I cannot pack the skillet or the one painting on the wall. The mirror will likely shatter, as will the few pieces of good crockery I possess. I take practical things. The brush and comb. The wedge of soap, wrapped in cloth, and my sewing kit. It doesn't add up to much, but I have neither the time nor the inclination to linger on how paltry our life is.

Hidden in a loose stitch of the bedding is the only item of value I possess. A small leather pouch containing hard currency. The small amount that I have managed to collect over the years, plus the wages earned from the tenant of Merryman croft. The earnings from Victor's anatomical studies, not my regular wages. All of that went into Mr. Tulloch's pocket, of course. It must sound crass to consider these coins more valuable than any personal items, but that is the cold truth of it. The risk I am taking is absolute, and the only thing that might stand between us and devastation is solid capital. Of course, Victor has wealth, but what if this adventure fails and he grows tired of me? What if, once we are away from this place and ensconced in some sunnier realm, the man might change his mind about a lover who towers a head taller than everyone in any given room?

With the children settled into bed, I pace before the hearth with a sickening churn in my belly. Am I really going to go through with this? How will I tell my husband I am leaving him and taking the children with me? How ugly will this get? There will be shouting and harsh words and, without a doubt, there will be violence. Mr. Tulloch's rage, once triggered, is a hot thing that cannot be put back into the bottle. It will also be tempered by his degree of inebriation. Perhaps I should go to bed and pretend to sleep until dawn? Giving Mr. Tulloch his bad news might be less calamitous when his head is throbbing from the vapors.

I settle on this plan as it is the sanest option, but luck has never been something I could count on. Just as I am undressing, I hear the door open, and the clumsy footsteps. My stomach lurches, but I will keep to my plan of telling Mr. Tulloch in the morning. The children are in bed, nothing is amiss to betray me. A night like any other in our drab circumstances.

He squints at me in surprise. "Were you waiting up for me?"

"I'm just going to bed now."

He shakes the rain from his coat. "Then my timing is impeccable."

Not this. He comes at me from behind with greedy hands and hot breath. I shrug out of his grip and tell him that tonight is not the night. He grins oafishly and comes at me again. I stop him cold at an arm's length.

"Stop it. I'm in no mood to be pawed at."

His face sours. "Why do you have to be so disagreeable all the time? Am I asking for too much? When did you grow so cold, woman?"

The cart rolls slowly downhill. If I do not stop it, it will be careening out of control. A few words of demure contrition might slow the cart. Begging forgiveness might chock the wheels and waylay the whole thing. Do it, I tell myself. Be contrite, avoid disaster. But there is another voice, rumbling underneath all the others, that wants destruction. Strike the match, this other voice says. Burn it all down.

"I am leaving in the morning," I tell my husband. "I am taking the children and we are leaving Eynhallow. For good."

His face drops, then he laughs at this. Slapping a knee, he says he's never heard anything so funny.

My gunpowder fizzles out. "Go to bed, Robert. I will wake you before we leave so you can say goodbye to the children."

I am not angry, nor am I sad. I am surprised at how peaceful I feel now that I have told him. It remains his choice to believe me or not, but I have done my duty. The relief it brings is remarkable. How long have I secretly despised my husband? Long enough for this moment to bring peace instead of tears.

My flat expression throws him off and his laughter droops. His eyes fall to the trunk, pulled away from its usual position at the foot of our bed. He throws the lid open, and blinks at what he sees. It takes a moment for the truth to pierce the vapors in his head.

And now here it is. The cart barrels downhill without a handbrake. His rage erupts, echoing through the stone cottage. He wags a fist in my face, demanding to know where I plan to go.

"Back to Kirkwall, is it?" he seethes at me. "To your father's house? Do ye think he'll let you disgrace his household?"

My face is stone. "I am not going to Kirkwall."

"Then where?" he snarls at me. "Who the hell is going to shelter a disgraced wife and her children? The workhouse?"

"We are going to the continent. Somewhere far away from here."

He's not as drunk as I had assumed, as he puts it all together very quickly—the continent, the foreigner in the rented cottage. His volume doubles, waking all the children now. He kicks over the trunk, spilling its contents on the floor. His fist lashes out, but I am already across the room and out of reach. He charges at me like a bull taunted by a crimson flag. Twice I dodge him, but his third attempt succeeds, and we crash to the floor. He is slow from the drink. I pin his arms and tell him to calm down, but he just bucks and thrashes until he throws me.

A plate is hurled at my head, a stool broken across my back. Mr. Tulloch's aim has always been deadly and the iron pot he flings connects with my brow. The pain is bright and blood flows into my eye.

He shrieks at me to get out. He calls me a whore and a tramp and pushes me to the door. All I want in this moment is to break his skull open, but the children are gawking at us with outsized, terrified eyes.

I stumble into the rain. The door slams behind me and I hear the never-used bolt slide home. My husband's rage overrides his superstitions.

The rain is cold. I duck into the shelter of the tattered peat shed and wonder what to do. I cannot go to Victor's cottage. I consider fleeing to Tom's. He would understand a nasty row between husband and wife, but he would have questions which I do not have the stomach to answer. The shed is dry enough so I will huddle here and shiver until dawn. A small sacrifice, considering how much is at stake. Tomorrow, my life will never be the same.

Something nibbles at my sleeve, pushing up against me for warmth. My sad shelter isn't so bad after all, with Daisy nuzzling close. I scratch her chin and that strangely divided eye of hers regards me with what I can only hope to be companionship. I suppose she has forgiven me for my harsh words to her.

I am almost content until a crack of light splits the night. My first assumption that it is lightning is wrong. The light flashes in a pandemonium of blue and green. And it issues not from the heavens, but here on earth. Just up the hill, over the Merryman croft.

CHAPTER XXX

Is the cottage on fire? What else could explain such uncanny light? The goat bleats as I rush out of the shed and race uphill. The driving rain blurs my vision and twice I slip, fall, and continue on. With the abode in view, I see that my alarm was misplaced for there is no fire. One window glows from within as a promising beacon against the night. Although cold and wet, I remember my promise to stay away from Merryman. I am unsure of what to do until a cry of anguish cuts through the wind. I double my pace and barrel through the door.

The first sensation is stench. A pungent mixture of brimstone and cinders. Underlying this is a worse smell, of something fermented and cloying. It is repellent.

The dying hearth renders just enough light to pick out a lone figure in a chair with his head in his hands.

"Victor, what's happened? Are you hurt?"

His head bobs up, confused. There is a dark smudge on his cheek. "Agnes? What are you doing here?"

"I saw the strange lights. I was worried." I reach out to clasp his hands, but I withdraw in disgust. "What is on your hands?"

"You mustn't be here, Agnes. I warned you."

He takes my arm to escort me out, but I shake out of his grip. His hands are red with blood and gore from fingertips to elbow.

"Again, with the blood? Victor, what in God's name is going on? And what is that horrible smell?"

He's not listening to me, driving me to the door, but I will not be shunted off. It pains me to see him so distraught, but my compassion is derailed by the sight of the open door behind him. The one that is off limits to me.

"What are you doing in there? What is this precious work you undertake? Tell me."

He will not. He begs me to leave, but I push him aside and march to the forbidden room. I should have listened to him.

I see, but do not understand. I hear and I smell, but neither faculty can make sense of the godforsaken tableau before me. The giant is here, his massive frame hunched over in these tight quarters. His head is bowed and his cadaverous, gray hand pets something on the slab table. A body, partially swathed in bandages and speckled with blood. Strange tubes pierce the limbs and torso, wires ensnare the head. But it does not move, this figure. Whoever this soul is, she is dead. The grotesque giant strokes the dead woman's hair with a loving hand. His head tilts and that ghastly face looks at me with those cadaverous eyes.

"Death, where is thy sting?" it says to me.

Why do I not run from the appalling scenario? What compels me forward to the dead woman on the slab? Do I already know who she is?

A tiny voice of salvation whispers at me to run and never come back. *Do not look. It will only break your heart.*

Another step and the true horror of it all is there to see. Splayed on the slab, her mouth gaping as if she is screaming against the defilement done to her.

"Oh God, Katie. What have they done to you?"

"Not enough," the creature rumbles.

My voice cracks. "You monster. Get away from her!"

The giant rises, his head strafing the ceiling timbers. "She was not strong enough. The creator has failed me."

My mind is already shutting down, unable to comprehend, let alone accept, the horrors inside the forbidden room. They have butchered and violated my dearest friend. I tear my eyes away from what they have done, only to discover more depravity. A small one, tucked neatly in the crook of the dead woman's arm.

The babe.

I scream. A shriek so raw and savage that it shatters a flask of green glass. The ogre stoppers his palms over his ears to save them from being ruptured by the sound.

My knees fail and down I go. But I cannot faint now. I have to get out of this torture room. Victor swims into view, patting my cheek to keep me from falling senseless.

The creature spews harsh words at Victor. The two shriek at one another, but I cannot make sense of their shrill words. The fiend says his claim still holds, the man curses the other to leave him in peace.

"Your obligation remains," says one voice.

"Are you blind?" says the other. "The process failed! There is no more."

The room is spinning. I cannot distinguish one combatant from the other.

"You have her."

"What? No!"

"She is strong. It will work on her."

The room falls silent, save for the drumming of rain against the shutter. And some other sound. Is that a baby crying?

"Do it, then. And be done with it!"

Darkness closes in. The last sensation is a hand around my throat. But whose hand? Dear God, won't someone see to the babe?

CHAPTER XXXI

I hear nothing, see nothing. A taste of salt. The cold.

CHAPTER XXXII

There is the dark and there is the cold. There is no beckoning light from afar nor a fall from grace. But there is pain. A thunderclap of white, unending pain. My head is afire, my ears baffled by a pounding pulse. A faint sound under it, perhaps. The wailing of a baby that will not stop.

Another thunderclap, so blinding that I feel my brains boiling inside my skull. My heart stumbles and stops, unable to find its rhythm. My fingertips itch and my ears prickle. Everything feels wrong. I sense pain, yet I cannot move. My ears detect sound, but it is baffled and mysterious. Is the babe still crying? I am blind and cannot speak. I don't even know if I am breathing, yet I must for I can think.

The awful wailing child finally fades away, replaced by the sound of a voice that grows louder. A man's voice. One that I should recognize, but I cannot place it. My father or son? My husband? I wonder if it is the boy who promised to rescue me, yet never came. What was his name?

Victor. His name is Victor. He wanted me to run away with him. He promised to take care of my children. That is who I hear. I cry out to him, but no sound issues from these lips.

His voice is feverish and hysterical, his words crazed. "In you, I have created a barbaric fiend. Am I now to form another? She might be a thousand times more malignant."

A second voice rises, this one unearthly and threatening. "Finish the task," it says. "Do it now."

"You have sworn to quit mankind, but she has not," argues Victor. "What if she refuses to go with you? You may even hate each other. You already loathe your own deformity. Would it not abhor you more in the female form? She may turn with disgust from you to the superior beauty of man, and you will be alone again, deserted by one of your own species."

"You made an oath to me," says the daemonic voice. I remember it now. The creature. "Finish your labors."

Victor's voice becomes shrill. "What if you thirst for children? A race of devils who would terrorize mankind. Who am I to inflict that on that world?"

"Fulfill your promise," cries the fiend. "Give her to me."

"No. Future generations will curse me for condemning the whole human race. I will not do it!"

New sensations rip into my flesh, hot and bright. A blade into my stomach, my ribs. There is a howl of rage and the sound of a struggle. Glass shatters, furniture topples.

The hateful voice again. "You dare break your promise? Do not dash my hopes now."

"Never will I create another like you," comes the reply.

The creature howls in anguish and rage. There is the sound of a fist pounding its breastbone. "Shall each beast have its mate and I be alone? Are you to be happy, while I am wretched?"

"Away from me!" cries the man I knew. "I will not do it!"

What follows is the abrupt crack of a pistol shot. The smell of gun powder fills the room.

"I shall be with you on your wedding night," says the fiend.

Another ruckus of tumbling, of glass breaking, and then all goes quiet. Even the rain has stopped.

This paralysis is torture. There is no sound, no movement for a very long time. Then the ripple of a sheet being unfurled. Hands push me over and my lifeless body hits the floor. I am wrapped in something and then dragged from the room, out of the cottage and across the heath. The culprit stops, and I hear him catch his breath before he resumes his toil. The sound of the shoreline grows near, and I am hauled into something hard. I hear waves lap against a wooden hull and the dip and rise of oars. A voice grunts and strains as my frame is rolled over the side and pushed overboard. The cold swallows me up and seawater salts my tongue. My canvas shroud unfurls in the current as I sink to the silty bottom of the sea.

The cold stings, the pressure throbs my ears. I feel a fish nibble at a toe, a crab scuttle through my hair. All else is darkness and salt.

CHAPTER XXXIII

How am I still conscious in this watery grave where the kelp is my shroud and the crabs feed on my lips? Is this Hell? It does not live up to its reputation. Why does oblivion refuse to come? I feel the sway of the current and the salt corroding my eyes. Every sense is grotesquely alert and tingling save for the means of locomotion or the capacity to scream. Oblivion, no matter how much I pray for it, does not come.

Hold now. A sound from above, like the splash of something hitting the water. The sensation of a hand gripping me by the hair and tugging me free of the kelp's grip. The pressure in my ears eases until I roll to the surface like driftwood. Something wades out of the water and hoists me over its shoulder. My head lolls as my long arms sway, fingertips brushing the grass.

I am unfurled like a drape onto a cold slab. I hear someone moving about clumsily and grunting in some toil. The terrible racket of a crank being turned faster and faster, triggering the crackle of some infernal engine.

Diabolical pain spasms every muscle. My blood is on fire, my brains sizzle. An unholy torment that rattles the meat from my bones. A scream, thwarted too long, finally erupts from my throat like a thousand unleashed banshees.

Light splits my eyes with clean pain, but it conjures shapes and shadows. I can blink. When my vision finally clears, I wish I was back on the bottom of the sea.

The creature towers over me in its corrupt flesh and appalling eyes. It caresses my hair and whispers repellent things into my blighted ear.

My limbs jerk into play, and I roll off the slab, scuttling crab-like to the far corner. The creature drops to one knee, a rancid grin stretching its terrible face.

"You live," it says. "Now I am the Creator."

"Get away from me." My own voice startles me. My vocal cords work, but this is not my voice. It sounds as vile as his does.

His hand reaches out to me with its greenish-gray flesh. "Do not be afraid. I am here to help birth you into this new life."

134

Its fingertips are cold marble against my brow. I swat it away. I scan the room with its cruel instruments and butcher's tools, but find no help, no savior.

"Where is Victor?"

"Gone," it says. "Abandoned his progeny. Again."

I slide further away from this monstrous thing that speaks riddles. "Did you kill him?"

The creature looks disappointed in me. "He is gone. Drifting out to sea."

The thing shuffles closer while I scurry back. I want to run but my limbs are clumsy and numb. I am swathed in bandages from throat to heel. Scraps of seaweed are caught in the linen.

"Do not be afraid," it says. "You will not suffer alone the way I did."

I scream at it to go away. I lash out to stop it from coming any closer. My hands. My God, my flesh is the same gray pallor as the ogre's.

"What did you do to me?"

"You were molded from clay and raised up."

"Stop speaking riddles! What did you do?"

The creature regards me with those soulless eyes. "Frankenstein thought he failed, but I could hear your heart beating. We are the same, you and I."

"I am nothing like you," I hiss. "You are a wretch. I am Agnes Tulloch. I am a wife and mother."

"Not anymore," it says. "You died. You live again. You and I are the only two of our kind. We do not possess names now."

I want to rip its damned eyes out, but I am graceless and slow. He catches my wrist with an iron grip.

"Be still and listen," the fiend says. "Ours is a story like no other."

I shake free of its grip and cover my ears. I do not want to hear what it has to say, but I cannot block out its terrible voice. The creature tells a story about a student of unhallowed arts, frenzied by ambition and hubris to unlock the secrets of nature and the mysteries of the divine. How this pale student pilfered graves and assembled a giant out of various body parts to which he infused the very spark of life. But when the student saw what he had brought forth, he fled in terror at the doll he had tailored. How the creation, abandoned and hated by everyone he encountered, fled into the forests and lived like the lowliest of animals. In time, this wretched creature came to learn of its origin and birth. How he is like a perverted version of the first man, driven from the garden to fend for himself. The lowly wretch sought out its creator and demanded a companion. A helpmeet like Eve, who was conjured from the rib of man. The creator relented, scurrying off to some hidden island to fulfill the obligation that was owed to its abandoned offspring.

I shriek at it to stop and curl into a snail on the blood-splattered floor, my head spinning from its awful, awful story.

The thing won't stop talking. How I wish to rip the tongue from its wretched head.

"This is how we came to be," it says. "You and I are our own unique and forlorn species. And like the first two, we have been cast out of Eden, but we will find a new garden. Far from here, to the wilds of the new world, where we will forge a paradise of our own."

My head is still a smoky haze, struggling to stitch one thought to the next. But the figures come together, and the sum is added up. The obligation that Victor spoke of, the promise that this creature clung to. It is me. I am the fulfillment of that vow. I am some profane Eve betrothed to this corrupt Adam.

I lash out again, but this time my limbs respond with frightening power. My very soul snaps, unleashing a daemon that tears at the wretch, ripping and gouging its despised flesh. My hands claw open its lip, my teeth chomp a finger. A bloodied surgical blade falls to the floor. I snatch it up and slash a great red stripe across its chest. The floor becomes slick with the creature's foul blood. When I slip and crash, the creature howls in anguish and flies through the casement into the night.

Flat in a pool of the thing's blood, I wonder how deeply I cut it and if it will die. A second, more horrid question occurs to me—can one kill that which is already dead?

CHAPTER XXXIV

The rain has stopped, but the wind will not relent. It flaps these loose bandages about me like tentacles. A tern calls to its mate somewhere on the shoreline. It is a familiar sound as I stagger down the pathway. Familiar is what I crave now, what I need. I've had my fill of horror and want no more.

Every muscle hurts, every bone grinds like grit against the millstone. Twice I fall to my knees, twice I grimace through the pain and push on. My only thought is of my children. I need to see their sweet faces and hear their honeyed voices. I need help. Dear God, I need help.

I will even be glad to see Robert's face, no matter the bitterness between us. After all this terror, all I want is to go home.

I do not realize my mistake until it is too late. I stagger through the door to find the glory of hearth and kin. The fire is soft, the children huddled around its glowing heart. Meg is asleep with her head in Kit's lap and Effie is snuggled in the arms her sister, Grace. Mr. Tulloch dozes in his favorite chair.

"Mother?" says Grace, peering through the gloom to see who has entered. The other three raise their heads and turn my way. I want nothing more than to pull them into my arms and never, ever let go. My heart thumps and swells as I stagger to them.

Sweet Effie is the first to scream. Her siblings quickly join her, their precious faces twisting into masks of terror as I step into the light. The younger three scurry behind their big sister and Grace herds them to the farthest corner.

My hands go up in surrender, to show I mean no harm. My voice croaks out in a terrible rasp, telling them that it is me, their mother. Why do they fright so?

Mr. Tulloch rouses from his sleep, confused and complaining. His expression turns to revulsion when it lands on me.

"Oh God," he says. "Oh, Dear Lord, save us."

It is only in this moment that I realize my error, but it is too late to rectify now. I beseech my husband that it is me, his wife, but he does not listen. He snatches up the poker and wields it like a sword, two handed and ready to punish.

The children's screams have harmonized into a single note of terror at the sight of their own mother. My words are useless.

"Begone, devil!" Mr. Tulloch puts himself between me and my children. He swings the poker to show he means business. "Get out, troll! Torment us no more."

The words tumbling out of my mouth sound strange and menacing to my own ears. My hands clasp together in supplication as I kneel before my family. I beg them to see that is me—their mother, wife.

Terror has baffled their ears against me. The children cower and hide their faces. Mr. Tulloch lets fly some Highland war cry as he strikes me with the iron rod. I beg him to see me now, but he responds with another swing that breaks against my temple. Panic erupts through the cottage, the goat bleats in distress. A pot of rainwater topples over as I retreat out the door and limp away. Westward across the heath I flee, to the most desolate corner of the isle until I collapse on the wet shale.

The horror of it is too painful to swallow. My own children do not know me. My husband thinks me a devil. I still do not understand what has been done to me, or what the Genevan and his creature have stolen from me. I claw at the earth and weep, but strangely, no tears fall. My eyes no longer shed tears. Another thing stolen from me.

The wind herds the clouds along, allowing the stars to come out. A crescent moon follows, its thin light raining down on my pathetic form, inert as a carcass in the clover. This is what I have become, a dead thing in a mad puppet show. I stare up at the stars and let myself feel nothing for a long time. The darkness turns blue then gray. Warmth from the east means the sun will come up soon. I cannot endure another scene like the one with my family, but where to go, where to hide? As loath as I am to return, the Merryman croft is the only shelter I can seek.

I approach it cautiously. No smoke issues from the chimney and the door stands open to the gusting wind. It appears to be abandoned. The fiend claimed that Victor had floated away in a skiff. Is that true? After the monstrous tale he told me, it is difficult to believe anything uttered from those black lips. Perhaps they are both inside, waiting to ensnare me like poachers.

The cottage appears empty. Tables and chairs lie belly up from my struggle with the creature and the fireplace is cold ash. The spare room is as empty as ever, the room with the slab is a riot of broken glass and scattered instruments. I close the door to this room, but the heavy stench leaks out through the cockeyed frame.

I should be safe here as no one ever visits the place. Matches lie scattered among the straw. I pick them out to renew the fire. On a peg hangs a cloak that I drape over my shoulders and pull tight. I am so cold.

Panic beats its wings in my belly, but I cannot think straight, nor choose a course of action. I can go neither forward nor backward because there is simply nowhere to go. There is always the sea, I suppose.

No, even that avenue of escape is closed to me. I did not drown when Victor flung me overboard. I simply sank to the bottom without the release of death. What in the name of God has the Genevan done to me?

The sun is up and warming the isle after the storm. I want to go out and let it steam the chill from my bones, but I mustn't dare being seen. The children will be up and about. Are they still quaking in terror from the ghost that burst into their home? Do they ask their father where their mother is? Grace will be banking the coals in the hearth to fix breakfast. She is quick and intuitive. Will she come here looking for me? I could not bear that.

A breadcrumb of memory brings me to the long table with its books and papers and glass vials. Hidden under a leather wrap of surgical knives is the thing I remember seeing. A small mirror that the tenant used for shaving. What it reflects now is unearthly and abhorrent. The flesh is a sepulcher gray, the pupils as milky as that of a dead fish. Seaweed caught in my hair. The looking glass holds no sign of Agnes Tulloch. It reflects only a ghoul, as hideous and malformed as the giant it was meant for. It is no wonder my children shrieked in terror. I am a troll come to life, a spook tale stalking the heath.

The glass is thrown into the fire. My vanity ceases to exist.

By midday, the smell in the croft is cloying. An overripe sweetness that reeks of only one thing and that thing is leaking out from under the door of the forbidden room. Oh God. More bits and drabs of last night come back to me. I do not want to go back into that chamber of horrors, but a terrible suspicion propels me forward. My hand on the knob, turning. The reek tumbles out like a thick fog. That godforsaken slab and the leather restraints, the surgeon's knives and rubber hose. Broken glass under bare soles, but I am numb to pain, it seems.

Where? Where are they?

In the corner, hidden under a canvas. When I tug the sail away, the smell is a blow to the face. My friend is a knot of bent limbs and white flesh. One eye open and staring, the mouth gapes as if Katie Kemp is still screaming in terror.

How cheap is life to someone who could do this? How entitled is the man who can treat another soul like a tool to be employed and then discarded when it breaks?

How could one be so blind as to love such a man?

Enough. There is work to do and I am happy to do it. Distraction and purpose will keep me from crumbling under all this wretched horror. But where is the babe? I roll Katie to one side, thinking the infant is trapped underneath, but it is not there. I dig through the broken clutter of the room, but the babe does not appear. Had I imagined it? I must have. The child is still in the coffin, left behind when its mother was stolen.

A cauldron of water is warmed over the fire and a handful of cloths are located on a shelf. I can find no soap. I lift my friend onto the slab to prepare her a second time, and wipe away the blood and the offal from her skin. I comb and plait Katie's thick hair. The bedsheets are stripped and used to swaddle the body. All there is to do now is to wait until nightfall before ferrying her vessel back to the graveyard.

It is a long wait. I sit at the window and look out on the plain below. I can see the islanders, down there, very small as they move about, but no one approaches the lonely croft uphill.

Behind me, a voice soft and as tender as it is familiar.

"Agnes, come," she whispers. "Come help me."

I turn to see Katie kneeling before the fire with the babe in her lap. She is rubbing its belly before the hearth.

"She is cold," my friend says. "Help me rub the warmth back into her. She will come back to me if we warm her."

My sanity is crumbling. How else to explain this vision of my departed friend. Again, she begs me to help her warm the babe. I tell her I am sorry. I tell her I cannot help. Katie cries, wipes her tears away. She tells me it is not fair.

I agree.

"Sleep now," I tell her. "Night will be here soon, and I will tuck you back into bed."

CHAPTER XXXV

Sundown bruises the clouds purple and the last of the gulls call out over the sound of the surf. The sliver of moon is even thinner tonight, but it provides enough light for my pilgrimage to the burial ground. I cradle the shrouded woman close to my heart as I make my way, whispering goodbyes into Katie's dead ear. She weighs next to nothing in my arms now. How heavy is a soul, I wonder.

The burden is laid gently in the clover, and I claw my hands into the turned earth. I know now why the grave was so haphazardly backfilled the last time I saw it. Victor and his monstrous puppet must have crept back the night of Katie's burial to dig her up. A horrid question bubbles to the surface, pausing my clawing hands. Did Victor rob the grave before or after we had lain together? Was there grave soil under his fingernails when he vowed to take us from this place? My mind is still too hazy to slot the events back in their proper order. Does it even matter now? No. Nothing so tawdry as romance matters now.

Back to digging with my hands. I waste a moment wondering what has become of the Genevan. Did he really drift off like the creature claimed? Drift off where? Has he fled back to the continent, back to his villa in Cologny? Perhaps he has already found another maiden to tumble, another eager ear into which he can breathe promises? How foolish I have been, believing the empty words of a nobleman. A leech, a parasite. Feckless and empty.

My fingers scrape wood. Digging to the bottom takes less time than I thought. My hands have always been strong, but this new brawn is something unforeseen, something unnatural. Clawing the dirt away, I lift the lid of the coffin. A simple casket, fashioned from the scrap lumber of the islanders. I am troubled to find it empty. Where is the infant? Is it hidden back in the cottage or was the child buried separate from its mother? My mind is still a wreck of scattered details and broken memories. I will search the cottage again when I return, but I cannot leave Katie lying out here in the open. I wipe my blackened hands before lowering my friend into the narrow box. With the lid squared, I crawl out and drag the loose soil back into the grave.

My palms tamp the earth flat, and I take another moment to right the listing headstone. I notice, almost idly, that a fingernail on my left hand has been ripped off from the digging. I did not feel a thing. Will it grow back or stay this bloody patch forever? I've heard that fingernails continue to sprout after death, growing into claws, but I do not know if this is true.

I wonder if I should say a few words now that Katie is back in her grave. What is there to say? A prayer? Whatever for? I have died and been risen. There is nothing after death but more death. Only a dunce would pray now. I bid farewell to my friend. There is nothing more to be said.

"Your kindness is moving," grumbles a voice on the wind.

I wheel about. The creature towers among the headstones, its stringy black hair blowing across that appalling face.

"Go away."

He nods at the grave before me. "She was your friend?"

The question knocks me back. "She was a kind soul. She did not deserve to be treated like rubbish."

He lowers his gaze. "We should not have mistreated her so. Ambition blinded us to that."

"Is that your excuse? You disgust me." I point to the grave. "Where is the child? It is not here."

The creature stares at me, but does not reply. It takes two steps, crossing the distance between us. I promise to claw his eyes out if he comes any closer. He begs me to listen to him.

"I will not," I reply. "Leave me in peace. Or run north and leap from the cliff."

The creature smiles at this, but it is the leer of a naked skull. "That solution does not work."

"Why can't you just leave me be?"

He reaches out his unnaturally long arm, extending a hand to me. There are suture marks where the fingers have been sewn onto the hand. "Come away with me. This is no place for you now. Come with me and we will find peace together."

Another promise, another offer of salvation from a man claiming to want to save me. My belly is full of these empty promises, and I vomit them back up.

"Where is Victor?"

"In gaol," he replies.

"Gaol? For what?"

Those dead eyes meet mine. "For the murder of his friend. An innocent man named Henry Clerval."

"I see." There is a tale within those words, but my heart is stony to it. I've had enough horror and misery for one lifetime. "Will he hang?"

"Yes."

"Very well," I say. My cloak flaps in the wind. I pull it tight and walk away.

His words billow on the gale, chasing me up the slope. "Have you returned to your family?"

My feet stop their tread. I refuse to look at him, but my silence is an affirmation.

"How did they receive you? With open arms or hatred and revulsion?" I hear his footsteps behind me. "That is the reception you will receive from every living soul you encounter. They will all despise you and fear you. Every hand will be raised against you. Save mine."

He comes about on the lee side of me, scrutinizing my stony face for a reaction. He won't get one.

"You and I are of the same clay," he pleads. "We were fated to be together. If not by the divine, then by the clockwork of Frankenstein's mechanics."

The wind flaps my hair about, obscuring the creature from my sight. He will not stop talking.

"Look at me now. I may be hideous, but my heart is as tender as any other. It responds to what is shown it. Rage, if that is what it is assailed with. But it will respond to love and comfort also. Our hearts are mirrors. They reflect back the purest of what we can be. Please, do not deny that to us both."

I remain mute, my eyes fixed on the dark sea. In lieu of a reply, he continues to study my features for a chink in my armor. For a glance or look of doubt that will signal to him that I have been won over. My eyes roll up to meet his, which he mistakes for acquiescence.

The giant reaches out to pull me into his massive arms. His chin angles like he means to press his black lips to mine. I take his head gently in my hands. Do I smile at him lovingly? I do not know. I dig my nails into his putrid flesh and rip both ears from his head.

His howl is the most unnatural cry I have ever heard. It echoes across the heath, sending a flock of sleeping birds to flight. The creature clasps his hands over his bleeding head and snarls at me, curses me. I look at the torn, misshapen ears in my palms and hurl them at the shore. Let the crabs have them now.

"You think I will love you because I was created to do so?" He staggers back and I follow him. "Should I faint with gratitude because you are willing to love me in all my wretchedness?"

My words are useless. This thing cannot hear me now. His features twist with pain and betrayal. Confusion, also. I follow as he stumbles to the rocky shore, his palms planted over his docked ears as if he cannot bear my words. He climbs into a skiff so small that his outrageous proportions threaten to capsize it. Blood trickles from his wounds as he takes up the oars and rows away from me.

CHAPTER XXXVI

There is something wrong with my thoughts. Memories fall out of my head like eiderdown from a pillow, leaving a flat, empty thing. I cannot recall my mother's name nor my father's house. Alone in the decrepit Merryman croft, I try to recall the story of the ghost that's said to haunt these walls, but I cannot. Was it about a sailor? A murder?

I suppose I am the ghost of legend now. I retrieve the shaving mirror from the hearth and shake off the ash. In the reflection is a ghastly wretch with cataract eyes and sunken flesh. I am both the ghost of Merryman and the mythic troll that lives in the caves on the Bowcheek.

At night, I leave the cottage to creep outside of my own home. I peer through the windows to watch over my children. They are not faring well. They barely speak and no one laughs. Meg no longer torments her brother and Effie prefers to be alone rather than curl into anyone's lap. Grace moves back and forth through the cottage, trying to perform my duties, which have landed on her shoulders. Mr. Tulloch sits in his chair, his features growing grim with every sip.

Twice I watch Grace drop into a chair and lay her head on the table. Unable to witness any more, I retreat back to the abandoned croft and sit unmoving like a helpless turnip. What can I do? I cannot help them. They will only shriek in terror if I step across the threshold of my own home.

Voices rattle me out of my woolgathering. Through the window I see two figures making the trek uphill. One is George Heddle, our neighbor. The other is my husband. Panic has me scrambling out of the window to hide behind the back wall. I wonder what has driven the two men to come calling at the rented cottage.

The men hallo the house and bang on the door. The hinges squeal open, and I hear their boots crunch the broken glass on the floor.

"Christ, look at the mess," says my husband.

"Something terrible has happened," is George's reply. There is fear in his voice. "Come away, Rob. Quickly now."

"Get a hold of yourself," says Mr. Tulloch. I hear his footfalls moving through the cottage. He calls out the name of the tenant as he searches. Then he calls for another.

"Agnes! Agnes, are you here?"

My belly flips.

"She's not here," says George. He never was the bravest soul. "Let's go home, Rob."

The rattle of a doorknob. "This door is locked," says my husband. "Help me get it open."

George argues against it, and Mr. Tulloch barks at him to man himself. I hear them shoulder the wood until the door snaps open, banging off the wall.

"Jesus Christ," cries my neighbor. "The place is a madhouse. What the devil was the man doing in here?"

"The stench," says Tulloch. "Something went ripe in here. And look there. Where did all this blood come from?"

"Saints above," declares George. "That's it. I'm getting the hell out of here."

The two men bicker over what to do. George refuses to spend another minute within the cottage. He stands out in the yard while Mr. Tulloch continues to search the place. I creep one eye over the windowsill and watch him rummage through the debris of the long table. The books hold no interest for a man who cannot read. Same with the loose notes in Victor's elegant script. He inspects the various bottles and flasks, smelling each one and wincing in disgust. He pockets a delicate flensing knife and a pair of scissors. His greedy fingers find the walnut box and flip the lid back. He scoops up the paper notes and shakes every last coin into his palm.

Outside the cottage, George nags him to hurry up. Mr. Tulloch ignores his friend and continues to root through the clutter. Something snags his attention, and I am surprised to see him leaf through the pages of a large book. Has he suddenly learned to read? I'm puzzled at what could possibly interest him so when I realize he is leafing through Victor's sketchbook. My mortification cuts sharp, remembering how many sketches Victor produced of me. My husband's face darkens as he scrutinizes each drawing. I watch his jaw muscle flex as he grits his teeth. I know that sign—a telltale mark of a rage about to erupt.

I snake one hand over the window casement to find the side table and push it over. The resulting crash makes Mr. Tulloch jump out of his skin at the strange noise. The ghost of Merryman croft is unhappy with this visitor and that reasoning plays out all over my husband's face. He dashes outside to collect his friend, and the pair march quickstep away from the lonely cottage.

146

When all is secure, I slip inside and take the sketchbook to the window where the light is best. It is strange leafing through all these charcoal renderings. Many of these sketches are anatomical studies of musculatures and ligaments, but some are more intimate, almost loving portraits. In one I repose like a Roman noblewoman on a divan, in another I appear as fierce and powerful as a Viking. A seductive temptress here, and an angelic martyr in another. Who is this woman in all these renderings? Is this really how the artist perceived me? For one small moment, my heart stops hating the man and a twinge of fondness returns. It is a bright and warm bloom, but it curdles quickly and does not last.

Night falls. My eyes seem better suited to the dark now. A little starlight is enough for me to navigate the ruined cottage. I dismantle the lamp, removing the delicate chimney and opening the bowl of seal oil. The greasy stench reaches my nose. I tilt the glass receptacle and leave a trail of the smelly liquid over the entire room. A match from the mantel is struck and set to the oil splatter. The flames lift and follow the trail I have made, spreading to the books and loose paper and fabric of the moth-eaten drapes. Soon the whole thing blazes up and I retreat outside to watch it all burn.

Cries from below as someone spots the blaze. Fire strikes true fear through every heart, and it brings them all running uphill to see the inferno. I withdraw and watch from a distance. The men have brought burlap sacks dripping from the rain barrels. There is nothing to be done to save the home, but when the fire fingers out to the dry heath, the men beat it down to prevent it from spreading. Fire is the great terror we all live with, for once it is out of control, it is ruthless and insatiable. The islanders gather around to watch the croft burn, but none seem sad to see the place go. Mrs. Dearness calls out to thank God when the first patter of rain falls around us. The people of Eynhallow retreat to their homes, grateful for the rain that will dowse the fire.

Myself, I am left unsatisfied, and retreat to the cliffs.

CHAPTER XXXVII

A cave in the treacherous cliff provides shelter. Twenty-Man Hole is a large cavern that is accessible from a cleft on the surface and a larger gap that opens onto the sea. I do not remember why it is called that, because there is not enough room for a dozen men, let alone twenty. I sit and watch the waves. Am I waiting for something? My mind is foggy much of the time now. My nature is changing also. I rarely sleep and do not feel much in the way of hunger. When my belly does growl, I snatch crabs from the rocky pool and suck the meat from the shell. My tongue is a dead thing. It tastes nothing but salt now.

Memories become as slippery as eels. Each one I try to recall and keep hold of just slips through my fingers. I am waiting for something but cannot recall what. Is someone supposed to come and take me away from all this? I cannot hold a thought for very long. Perhaps the grave worms are already eating my brains.

My days are spent inside the cave, but my nights are occupied with stalking the island. I linger outside my home, watching my family through the slats in the shutters. They are not doing well. A sort of squalor has taken over the cottage. Grace does what she can, but it is too much for one girl. Mr. Tulloch does not lift a finger to help. He sits before the fire and drinks his drams and complains to his children. Daisy the goat has free reign, roaming about the cottage like a family pet. When Effie asks when mother is coming home, no one answers her.

I am haunting my own life. It is a confounding sensation.

On the third night of my vigil, I become careless and am spotted by someone. Not one of my children, but Nelly Heddle of all people. I don't see her until it is too late, but I hear her scream as she comes up the pathway. I flee to a distance and crane my ear. Mr. Tulloch and the children run outside to see what the disturbance is about. Nelly is in tears, claiming to have seen a ghost skulking through the night. Mr. Tulloch puts an arm around her and leads the rattled woman home. He tells Grace to herd the children inside and lock the door.

Crawling out of my cave the following night, I find a hubbub stirring among the islanders. I watch Mr. Tulloch march the children outside where they meet up with Tom and the six Kemp children. Together they follow the path down the slope to the Dearness abode, where the Heddle family have already arrived. A rare evening gathering of islanders, but it is neither a feast day nor harvest time. The Dearness cottage has a window of leaded glass that affords a view to the hearth room where Mr. Dearness arranges enough chairs and benches for the adults to sit. His wife serves tea with oatcake. It is clear from the grim faces that this is not a pleasant social gathering.

Nelly is still agitated by the apparition she encountered. She fusses and fidgets while Mr. Dearness thanks everyone for coming and rambles on in his obtuse manner about why they have gathered tonight.

"Can we please get to the point, Mr. Dearness," Nelly interjects, cutting off the parson. "We are not safe on this isle. Something is here."

The parson smiles cheerily and bumbles along. "Yes, well, I thought we might first discuss the fire—"

"Something is on the island," Nelly cuts in again. "I saw it last night. I know not if it was a troll or a spirit, but it was real."

Her husband makes a polite cough to cover his embarrassment. "Well, we're unsure exactly what was seen."

Nelly is adamant. "I saw it! You all know me, you know I am not one for fanciful thinking. But this thing was terrifying. It stalks the island."

Tom Kemp nods along with her statement. "My Katie saw it, too," he says. "She didn't get a clear look, but she said it was frightening."

The discussion divides the room between those who believe Nelly's claim and those who do not. Mr. Tulloch's sour expression reveals which side of the debate he falls on. This comes as a surprise, since he and the children were terrified by my appearance that first, awful night. Why does he stay silent on the matter?

I watch Grace edge closer to the inner circle of adults. The girl clearly wants to speak up but is fearful of her father's reaction. She tugs his sleeve and whispers to him, but he dismisses it and shoos her back to the other children.

George is stuck somewhere in the middle, skeptical about the claim, but obliged to side with his wife. Mr. Dearness tries his best to mediate, but he is unable to get anyone's attention, let alone come to a consensus. Poor Mary Dearness looks terrified, her teacup rattling against the saucer.

Nelly Heddle's patience runs out. She stamps her heel on the floor and gets to the point. "We are not safe here. We must do something."

"Let's not lose our lids just yet, Nelly," tuts Mr. Dearness.

Mrs. Heddle will not be patronized. "We all know the stories about this place. Trolls have haunted this isle since the Norsemen were here. Have we done something to anger them? Is that why they burned down Merryman croft? Are they responsible for Agnes' disappearance? No one's seen her in days. Nor the foreign man."

The sound of my own name startles me. The fact that Nelly is the one to bring it up is even more unsettling. My husband has said nothing about it. He still does not address it.

"There is no evil spirit, Nelly," he says. "Can we dispel with that notion, please?"

Mrs. Heddle fires back. "You didn't see it! If you had, you would be of a different mind." Nelly covers her hands over her mouth, her eyes drawing large. "I fear I have caused this. I was unkind to poor Agnes. More than once. Did my cruelty cause this spirit to come snatch her away?"

This stings as much as it surprises. The unkindness cuts both ways and my shame over it runs to the quick. Why did Nelly not show this tenderness of heart when it mattered? Only now that I am gone does it emerge, when it does me no good. It confounds me.

Mr. Tulloch raises his voice. "For Christ's sakes, Nelly. She wasn't taken by some ogre."

"Robert," George warns. The two men are best friends but there are lines one doesn't cross in public.

My husband glowers at being scolded, but Mr. Dearness furrows his brow like he's snagged a fish on the line. "Do you know something we do not?" he asks my husband. "Come, come, Robert. Out with it."

Mr. Tulloch rubs his jaw and fidgets in his seat. He can be a clam when it comes to the truth, but all eyes are on him now. "My wife was not taken by some monster," he gruffs. "Nor was the missing tenant. The two of them ran off together."

A chorus of gasps and whited faces, followed by a flurry of questions. Is this true? How does he know this? Agnes would never do such a thing.

Tulloch wrings his hands. I can tell he desperately wants a drink, but our parson is an avowed teetotaler who does not permit the stuff under his roof. "She told me. We had an argument, and Agnes informed me that she was leaving the island forever. She ran off to the foreigner's cottage. In the morning, they were gone."

The questions fire again, but they quickly twist into condemnation. How could a mother abandon her own children? What kind of monster would do such a thing? How will they survive without a mother? Who knew the tall woman was so grandiosely selfish? Did she lose her mind?

My heart slows, cold as November rain.

It is a half-truth, but there is no one inside the Dearness cottage to advocate on my behalf. I am tarred and feathered in absentia, hung like a criminal. I watch in disgust as my neighbors pat Mr. Tulloch on the shoulder and offer him condolences for his poor treatment. In the corner, the children have fallen silent, craning to hear every scrap of scandal. Grace lowers her head in shame.

Effie, who has always had the ears of a rabbit, turns to the window, and looks directly at me. I recoil and run away.

My betrayal is complete, my condemnation ironclad. I stagger across the heath in a tempest of bubbling rage and clammy despair. I truly become the tormented spirit of legend, howling into the wind. My steps lead all the way to the cliffs of the Bowcheek. A straight plunge to the crags fifty feet below. Painted into a corner, I see no other path to take.

I jump.

CHAPTER XXXVIII

The pain is spellbinding and without end. The simple act of opening my eyes causes me to lose consciousness again and again. I hear the water lap against the rocks and the cries of gulls overhead. The wheezing, gurgling draw of my own breath is torture.

I don't know how many days pass before I can simply lift my head. Three, maybe four. When I finally manage, I look down at my body like it belongs to someone else. One leg is broken so badly that a bone extrudes from my shin. The other is twisted under me. Shattered ribs roll loosely in my chest as I breathe, and my left arm is snapped at the shoulder.

There is no blood. The sea washed it away days ago. Again, the taste of salt is everywhere. God, I am thirsty.

The crabs come out. An armada of the little beasts scuttle all over my broken frame. I watch them peck and prod with their little claws as the devils eat my dead flesh. How the worm has turned, I think, as my food source now feasts on me.

It takes two whole days to claw my way up from the craggy rocks and drag my broken body into the cave. My howls of torment echo through the stony chamber of Twenty Man Hole like a chorus of deranged cupids. When my anguish subsides, the ever-present wind blows through the cave and whistles through the fissures of the rocks. And on the wind comes the tormented wail of a baby crying. Katie's unnamed child. I never did find it. My mind becomes more unmoored each day, I fear.

The filthy bandages that swath my limbs prove useful. My teeth grind as I re-apply them, using the linen to cinch wounds and strap the bones back into place. With this accomplished, I collapse and do not move for another three days. My heart continues to beat through all of this. My blood, if it can still be called that, pumps and courses. What in the name of God has Victor Frankenstein done to me? A single thought nestles in my mind like a worm, eating away all other thoughts. It is an obscene and blasphemous notion, but it is the only conclusion to be made.

I cannot die.

CHAPTER XXXIX

Three days and nights pass before I crawl out of my lair to resume my nightly hauntings. My back is bent, preventing me from standing straight, and my stride is hobbled by the broken leg. I move with the same lurching gait as the creature did.

I watch my family through the shutter slats. The Tullochs have never been prosperous, but the conditions were never squalid either. That is not the case now. The cottage is in shambles and the children go about filthy and sad. Grace does her best to scrub their grimy faces, but her siblings revolt and fight back. The girl has aged years in my absence. There is no spark in her eyes now.

Their father is of no use. He is out until late, and when he returns, he drops into his chair and sips from the pewter cup. Sometimes he raises his voice. Two nights ago, he berated Grace because his supper was cold. It took everything I had to refrain from bursting through the door to murder the man.

When the sun is high, I stay hidden in my lair, but on darker, overcast days, I venture out to watch from afar. Today is such a day, with a wind that pushes and pulls and a sky pouting with rain clouds. Observing from a distance, I watch Kit help his sister stack fresh peat into the shed while Meg feeds the hens. We have lost two of them since the night I disappeared. Daisy the goat bleats at the girl for attention, but Meg no longer rides the animal like she used to. I look for my youngest, but do not see Effie anywhere. Is she ill again?

I spot her halfway across the isle, headed toward the ruins of the old kirk. None of her siblings notice the wee one wandering off by herself, so I retreat to the westerly shore and follow the child at a distance. I am lucky in that the fishermen keep their boats moored this day. The winds make the channel too dangerous to venture out. Twice I watch the wind blow little Effie down. The child picks herself up, brushes the grass from her knees and ambles along to the stone ruins. Why is she going there? I do not like the thought of her out of sight and out of mind of her siblings. Mishap and injury come too easily to children on this island.

The ruins are something of a maze, with chambers within chambers. Roofless, the walls are high enough to hide from the outside world. Even for one as tall as I am. I hobble through a low arch and follow the sound of my child's voice. She sings as she makes her way through the maze of sandstone. I find her in the innermost chamber, sitting in the dry grass with her back to the entrance. Euphemia Jane draws something from a pocket, but I cannot see what it is until she turns. A length of paper that Effie unfolds and stares at like a student studying a lesson. I have taught all my children their letters, despite my husband's grumbling. Grace took to it easily, and Kit struggled a little, but he is literate. Meg fought me the whole way, but Effie's education has barely begun. I wonder if Grace has added her little sister's education to her list of chores now that their mother is gone.

I am mistaken. It is not a sheet of letters, or a leaf torn from a book. It is a drawing done in charcoal on brown paper. The portrait of myself done in Victor's deft hand. Effie stares at it like it is a puzzle to be solved. Inside my chest comes a sharp sound like that of a twig snapping in winter. My hand is quick to stifle the sob bubbling up.

But not quick enough.

I recoil when the child twists around. Her voice is fragile against the rushing wind. "Who's there?"

It is foolish to linger. I should flee before she finds me, but it has been so long since I have heard her voice. I cannot leave.

"I know it's you, Meg," she says. "Don't try to scare me."

The girl is already getting to her feet, but I do not flee. I remain as foolish as a stump and let the catastrophe unfold. I pull the cloak tighter, draw the hood down. The child rounds the corner, her eyes rising to the figure towering over her.

Fear whites her eyes, but she does not scream. The gentle brow furrows, the lips purse the way they do when she is concentrating. The two of us are motionless, as if daring the other to speak first. A gull passes overhead.

"Mam?"

Another snap inside my ribs. I didn't think there was anything left to break in there. The child rushes at me, but I raise a hand in warning.

"Stop."

Effie does what she is told, but she frowns at me.

"Where did you go?" she asks. "Why do you not come home?"

This is too much to bear. Even the pain from my suicide jump is nothing like this.

"I cannot come home. I am sorry."

"But we miss you." Her face pinches tight. She is trying not to cry. "We all miss you. Father, too. Even Daisy misses you."

Why did I not run when I had the chance? Did I think this would be a heartfelt reunion?

"I'm sorry, pet. I miss you, too, but I can't come home."

Euphemia puts up a brave fight, but the tears come all the same. She knuckles them away and says she doesn't understand. She wants to know why I left them. She asks if she did something wrong to make me go away.

I bend my broken leg, dropping to a knee so that our eyes align. "You did nothing wrong. Not you, nor sisters or brother. Do you understand?"

She drags a sleeve under her nose. "Meg said you died. In the fire."

"Your sister just wanted to scare you. You know how she is."

The girl narrows her eyes, trying to get a better look at what is under this hood. "Did you die? Is that why you went away?"

My heart is too raw to compose a compassionate fib. "Yes, Effie. But that doesn't mean I do not love you or think of you every day."

"No!" The girl stomps her foot. "I want you to come home. Everyone is sad. You must come home!"

It is enough to knock me down, this child's grief and frustration.

"Listen to me, Euphemia. Know that I will always watch over you. Your mother's spirit is never far from you and your sisters and brother. Chin up now. Be a strong girl."

She sniffles. She dries her eyes and stands straight as a pin.

"Run home now. Grace will worry about you. But tell no one you saw me. They won't understand and will say you're telling stories. This is to be our secret."

"Yes, Mam."

"Promise me."

"Yes, Mam."

I remind the child to listen to her big sister. I tell her it is not fair that Grace must work so hard now. I tell her to remind her brother not to fight with his sister. There are a thousand more things I want to say, but I stifle myself.

"Remember what I said about keeping this secret. Can you do that?"

"Yes, Mam."

"Good. Off you go," I say. "And tell Meg to keep her pet out of the house, please."

She scampers off, her little legs scissoring through the grass. I retreat to the shore. What foolishness have I wrought, asking a child of four to keep a secret like this? My brains must have dashed all over the rocks when I jumped to my death.

CHAPTER XL

To her credit, the child manages to keep her secret for most of the day, but she grins like a kitten in cream the whole afternoon. Her siblings pester her about what is so funny and why is she acting so strange. Effie's cheeks puff out as she holds her breath.

When a debate ensues about how to fillet the skate, Effie says that's not how Mother does it.

"Mother is gone," Grace replies impatiently.

"No, she's not," replies the child. "She's watching over us."

Observing from the window, it is now my turn to hold my breath.

"Don't talk like that," scolds her brother.

Effie stamps her little foot. "It's true. I saw her."

Grace glances to the chair where her father sits idle in his thoughts. She shushes her siblings. "Pipe down."

Mr. Tulloch stares into the fire, sips from his cup. A shudder runs through him and he sloppily barks my name, telling me to quiet the damn baby. He can't take any more of its awful keening. Lord only knows what he's hearing in his state. The wind ferries its terrible messages to us all.

The children stiffen at his voice and fall silent. When their father settles, they resume their whispering.

"You're such a little liar," says Meg. "Mother is gone."

Effie's face blows red, hissing at her brother and sisters. "You're wrong. I saw her. She spoke to me."

The older three huddle around the baby, telling the child to stop telling stories. It's rude. Effie stands her ground.

"I saw her. She doesn't look like herself," the child reports. "But she doesn't look like an angel, either. She watches over us now. I swear."

Grace tugs her little sister's sleeve. "Enough fibbing, Effie. You'll upset everyone."

"But I'm not. She said it's not fair that you do all the work now, Grace. She sees how you work to keep us all happy."

My eldest daughter becomes stone. Her eyes glisten and she turns away quickly.

Effie turns to Meg. "She said to keep Daisy outside. This isn't a barn." To her brother, she says, "And Mam said you need to help Grace. You're not the man so don't act like it."

What have I done? Grace takes the child by the shoulder and shakes her. "Hush now. Don't let Father hear you say such things."

Their father has the ears of a dog, hearing only what it chooses to. The food dish, but not the command. Lifting his head from his reverie, he leans forward to glare at the brood. "What's that now? What am I not to hear?"

"It's nothing, Father," insists Kit, looking as guilty as a fox.

"Mam's spirit watches over us all," declares Effie. "Even you, Da."

Their father's elbow slips from the table, his glower deepening. "What the devil did you say?"

The older three instinctively pull the youngest behind them as if to hide her. Meg says Effie is reciting rhymes. Grace explains she had a bad dream is all. Kit quivers. He knows his father's sharp hand better than any of them.

Little Euphemia never did know when to pipe down. She prattles on, condemning them all. "Mam is with us. She will protect us all."

The chair topples as Mr. Tulloch launches to his feet. "You are never to say her name in this house again! Do you understand? The woman abandoned us. She is dead to me, and I'll not have her mentioned again!"

My hand is on the window latch, ready to throw it open. How many times have I seen my husband boil over into rage? I will not let the children suffer it, but to intervene would mean frightening them all.

The baby of the family will not relent. She insists her mother is here among them until Grace slaps her palm over the girl's running mouth. It is too little and far too late.

Mr. Tulloch kicks the chair across the room and clenches his fists. "The woman is a whore, do you hear me? I'll not hear another word otherwise. She is a faithless harlot!"

The man lumbers toward the cowering children, his hand closing into a fist. Grace pushes them all behind her and steels herself for the blow.

Boom. Tulloch startles, the children squeal in surprise. All turn to see the side table under the window has crashed to the floor of its own accord. As if toppled by a ghost.

158

Grace pushes the others to a corner far out of reach of their father's rage. Mr. Tulloch's eyes dart back and forth, searching for an enemy or a reasonable explanation. Finding neither, his attention swings back to the children. His fury clicks back into place like a gear finding its tooth.

A second jolt as a stone-rattling boom echoes through the house. The door this time as something thunders against it hard enough to loosen the hinges. Screams from the children, curses from the father. Even the goat bleats in panic. Robert marches for the entrance and flings the door back.

There is nothing to see but twilight shadows against the ragged horizon.

Rattled, Mr. Tulloch barks at the children to go to bed. "No prayers this night," he tells them. "Just hop abed and be quiet."

From the window, I watch him snatch his coat from the peg and tell the children he is going to visit George. Grace says goodnight, looking very much relieved. The broodlings scurry to get to bed as their father stomps out of the cottage. With the hinges broken, the door no longer slots into its frame as before. Mr. Tulloch shoulders it shut, curses, and marches south toward the Heddle cottage.

I follow.

Twenty paces on, he stops and looks behind him. All there is to behold is the silhouette scape of the land against the sea. Seeing nothing that should cause his nape hair to bristle, he spits and continues on. I follow him at a distance, making just enough noise to make him stop and turn again.

"Who's there?"

The gust answers, blowing downwind toward him. I watch his nostrils flare as he smells something in the air. His eyes remain useless in the gloaming. He bellows again, demanding to know who shadows his tread, but his bluster is not half so bold. The darting eyes and bobbing apple of his throat betrays how unnerved he is.

Good.

He doubles his pace, hurrying to the welcoming squares of light from the windows of the Heddle cottage. Safety and warmth await, along with the clink of a bottle neck against a cup.

Now is the time to strike. As hobbled as I am by the broken leg, I move far quicker than I ever did in life. Circling around, I block his path and wait for his eyes to find the dark figure standing in his way.

His face blanches white, eyes bald in terror. He even manages to utter a cry for mercy in a quivering tone.

Eynhallow

One blow is all it takes to knock him flat to the ground. He wheezes in panic as I drop onto him, pinning his arms under my knees.

"Look at me, Robert." My voice is as unnatural as my appearance now. "Do you know me?"

His head shakes back and forth in a deranged panic. My hand clamps his jaw to still him.

"Say it," I tell him. "Say my name."

He stammers and sputters, terror stealing his voice. The third attempt brings my name to his lips.

"Agnes," he mewls. Tears fall as he clamors on. "Agnes, Agnes, Agnes. Please don't kill me."

"Why would I kill you? Our children depend on you. Man thyself and protect them. From yourself most of all. Do you understand?"

He begs for his life. He pleads with me to let him go. Wrong answer.

"Never lay a hand on them," I spit into his face. "Promise me or I will tear out your heart and feed it to you."

He swears. He swears on his God and his mother. I get to my feet, releasing him. The wretch lies there panting in terror.

"Go home."

He scampers to his feet and runs breakneck into the dark. A noise rises from behind me. I turn to see the door of the Heddle cottage swing open. George Heddle peers into the dark, alerted by the ruckus outside his home.

I shriek into the night with an ear-splitting howl. Mr. Heddle slams the door shut and shoots the bolt home. Everyone on Eynhallow locks their doors now.

CHAPTER XLI

Two days on, I watch my family drag the battered sea chest down to the shore. Tom Kemp's boat is waiting. They are leaving the island of Eynhallow.

Last night's haunting was different. I stood outside the casement and watched my husband mummer my own actions from a fortnight ago. He and the children pack their clothes and our meager belongings into the old trunk. They take only what is necessary, what will fit into the one good trunk that we possess. Other things, that can be sold if need be.

There is, of course, his little trove hidden behind a loose stone in the wall. He reaches into the crevice and withdraws a leather pouch of coin and notes. I am shocked to see the sum he has amassed. A small portion of this is the wages that the foreigner paid, but where on earth did the rest of it come from? I had no idea he had accrued this much. Whenever I had begged him in the past to spend a little on some necessities, Mr. Tulloch would plead poverty and withdraw only lint from his empty pockets. But all this time he was sitting on this little treasure horde. Why am I surprised?

A knock at the broken door startles everyone, but it is only George Heddle. The neighbor is upset at Tulloch's hasty decision to leave. Where will he go? What will he do and how will he provide for his family? Mr. Heddle begs Robert to reconsider, but my husband will not change his mind.

Mr. Tulloch pulls his friend aside to speak out of earshot of the children. He whispers to George that the ghost is real and that the island is truly haunted. Nay, he corrects, it is cursed. He advises George to abandon this place also before shooing the man out the door to continue packing.

Come dawn, my family is at the shore with their trunk and other paltry belongings. I watch them load into the Kemp skiff and push off. Tom drops the oars and rows for the mainland. All my children are crying, but Meg is the most heartsick in this moment. She begged her father to bring her pet, but he said they could not take the goat. To console her, he tells the child that Mr. Heddle will look after Daisy now, but I doubt this is true.

Daisy the goat stands on the beach and, like me, watches the Tulloch family bob on the waves. I turn away and creep back along the western shore to my cave. If I could weep, I would, but my eyes no longer produce tears and there is nothing inside my breast that feels anything now. If one was to poke a hole between my ribs, they would find a little loose dirt and nothing more.

A week later, the Kemp family is next to pack their things and leave. I lurk outside their cottage and eavesdrop as Tom explains to Mr. Dearness his reasons. Without Katie, Tom cannot properly care for his six children in these harsh conditions. His late wife's brother is running the family farm, but he could use some help. Tom will take his brood to Stromness where they will have a better chance at thriving. Mr. Dearness does not want to see the man go, but he cannot argue his reasons. I watch from afar as Mr. Kemp loads Katie's children and their goods into his boat. All the islanders come out to wave goodbye. Daisy the goat leaps into the skiff, but Tom lifts her back onto the shore. Willmouse and his siblings wave again as their father mans the oars. The residents turn and walk home. The goat remains on the beach, bleating plaintively.

The animal will not come close. She is never far away, but if I try to scratch her chin or pat her head, Daisy shies away. She's wary of me now, as I suppose she should be. But she's lonely and never strays too far from my side.

As the days pass, I find myself resenting the other islanders. A dark and unkind notion fills me, and I begin to haunt the holy isle in earnest. I rattle doors and scratch at the windowpanes. My hands rip up vegetable patches and snap the necks of yardfowl. I howl into the night and listen to the islanders whimper and pray to the Almighty to save their souls from the spiteful troll that torments them.

Hugh and Mary Dearness are the next to abandon the island. The Heddle family follow suit three days later. While Nelly and her sons drag their belongings down to the shore, I watch George stride out to the pasture where the horse is grazing. There is a flintlock in his hand. The crack of gunfire sends birds flapping to the air, and then Mr. Heddle joins his family as they load the boat. When they push off and row away, I rise from my hiding spot and walk down to the beach where they alighted. Nelly clutches her children close when she sees, for the second time, the ghost of Eynhallow. She pleads with her husband to row faster. George blanches in fright and puts his back into his labor. The current is rough this day. It carries them down the mainland coast, far from their intended landing at Tingwall dock.

Daisy watches from a small hillock before turning her eyes to me. We are the last residents of Eynhallow now.

I pass the day watching the sea. It is almost supernatural how the twinkling waves lull me into a thoughtless stupor. The deserted island is quiet now that the Orkneymen have left. There is only the wind which cannot make up its mind between a benign breeze and an indignant gale. It carries the sound of the waves and the warbles of the birds overhead, the bark of a seal sunning itself on the beach. But there is another, detestable sound that rips open my peaceful stupor like a candle flame to the fingers. That awful keening of the baby. It is never far away, whispered on the wind, but I took it simply as proof of my deteriorating faculties. It is Daisy who proves otherwise, as I see her tall ears twitch at each mournful cry.

No, no, no. We mustn't think that. It is too horrific to consider. Katie's own words come to mind that day she clamped my wrist tight. *Something is on the island with us.*

All the same, I rise to my feet and stride across the heath, trying to locate the source of that awful sound. Again, it is the goat who shows the way. She follows me along until we are close to the western shore before traipsing away north towards the Bowcheek. I let her lead the way to an outcropping and look down to the waterline.

It is a terrible and unholy thing to behold.

CHAPTER XLII

I pray that my eyes are playing tricks on me, that the light on the water is casting things that are not really there. But that is not true. It lies on the wet shale, rolling to and fro with each swell and draw of the waves. It squirms and cries, seawater washing over its pinched face. Pale as a fish belly, it glows against the black stone and dark water. How long has it been down here, trapped on the rocks like this? How has it not been snatched up by some hungry fish? Perhaps the beasts know it is an unnatural thing and stay well away from it. Abandoned and cast out, it wails and wails.

Katie's poor doomed child. Or it was that briefly, now it is something else. Like myself and the abhorrent giant with the lifeless eyes. Dead, and yet it moves somehow. A thing without a name. Unholy and pathetic.

Why had he done it? I understand now why he subjected me to his infernal procedure. I was meant to be a mate for the loathsome wretch Victor had created. But why resurrect the babe? Was it some perverse curiosity on his part? His hubris? I wonder if it was Victor at all. Perhaps the creature did this to the child. A wife and child, all manifested at the snap of his fingers to worship and adore. I think I am going to be sick.

My approach is clumsy and slow on the slurry pebbles. The infant lies helplessly, but it must sense my presence as its wails double in volume. Tiny hands of grey flesh grasp at the air. The shrill cry shudders instinct to life and, without thinking, I reach down and lift it from the cold water. Its face pinches into a furious grimace as it shrieks and cries. It squirms in my arms, nestling into me to suckle. God help me, I let it. I have nothing to give it, no milk to provide, but still I allow it to latch on. Toothless though it is, it bites with the ferocity of a lamprey until I bleed and it nurses my poisoned blood in place of milk.

Everything about this is wrong. This dead, yet, not dead, infant should not exist. No soul should be trapped in such a blasphemed vessel as this. I let the wee thing suckle a moment longer, probably the only comfort this creature has ever known. And then, with a sharp twist of my wrist, I snap its neck.

164

It goes limp in my hands. And then the thing I am dreading occurs. It spasms to life, the little limbs convulsing and already the puckered mouth searching for comfort. Like me, it, too cannot die. The cruelty of it beggars belief.

What do I do? Do I dash its brains against the rocks or bludgeon it with a stone? I cannot let it suffer like this. A sound above me turns my attention. Daisy the goat looks down from the rock above, bleating at me as if to hurry me to some resolution. I climb back up and carry the tiny thing across the heath to the nearest croft in sight. The parson's home.

The peat shed is well stocked. I pile it high in the yard and gather reeds and sticks for kindling. Inside the cottage, I find a box of matches on the mantel and the lamp on the window sill. The oil will ensure the bonfire rises to life quickly.

The babe shrieks as I tear it from my cold nipple and lay it gently on the funeral pyre. The match is struck and the oil blazes up hungrily until the entire mound of peat is on fire. The thing cries and cries and will not stop. I clamp my palms over my ears and step back from the heat.

For three days and three nights, I do not let the fire go out. I empty the peat shed of its supply and when that is gone, I break apart the table and the chairs to keep the fire blazing. The wind saws the flames east, then north, flickering hot embers into the sky and across the heath. The cries of the infant did not stop until the second day of the pyre. Daisy bleats from afar, wanting nothing to do with this profane fire.

On the third day, I spy a boat on the water. A sturdy skiff from the mainland with two men at the oars. The fire must have been spotted from the far shore and raised questions about its origins. These two men have come to investigate its cause. I watch them row to the beach and splash ashore, but I do not want them here. I rise and cross the heath to greet them. One halloes from a distance and the other waves to me. Their greetings change to horror when they get a closer look at my form striding toward them. They quickly push off again, leap back into the boat and row away. The ghost of Eynhallow does not welcome visitors now, and the men oblige.

When the fire runs its course, I sift the ashes for anything left behind but there is nothing but gritty flakes and white powder. The soft bones have been incinerated completely. I claw a hole in the earth with my fingers and rake the ashes into it, burying all trace of it.

My sanity falters after this. I spend days watching the sea, losing track of time and weather. Rain, shine, or hail, I remain as still as a stump, gazing out over the face of the water. What am I looking for? Sometimes I do not remember. Is it Robert or the lad who promised to rescue me so long ago? Is it the man from Geneva or the terrible giant with the dead eyes? Daisy bleats nearby, occasionally nibbling my sleeve, but she still refuses to be scratched. I sit motionless for so long that lichen creeps from the rock to my flesh.

I return to my own cottage and build a fire, but there are too many wistful memories caught in the cobwebs. I leave and never go back. I wander the shoreline before returning to the cave. Time loses all meaning. Days, months pass without notice. Seasons turn in and shuffle out. Daisy's beard grows white. Her bleating is not so plaintive these days. One winter morning, I notice that I do not hear her familiar warble and go looking for the animal. I find her tucked into a corner of the old church ruins. She had come here to escape the knifing wind and expired in the night. I am sad for a little while, and then I forget all about her.

I forget more and more as each season turns to the next. Names and faces scatter like straw on the wind, the past crumbles away. I stare at the sea for days and weeks, trying to remember what I am looking for.

CHAPTER XLIII

A boat appears on the sea, bobbing in the chop. A lone oarsman struggles to propel the craft through the current to the shores of Eynhallow. Is this the person I have been waiting for?

So many things I don't remember now. How I came to be here or who I am. I had a name once, I am sure of it, but it has been so long since anyone uttered it. A jangle of names come to mind like Katie or Grace or Nelly, but which one is mine? Does it matter?

The skiff beaches on the pebbly southeast shore. The oarsman splashes into the water, hauls the boat up, and surveys his landing. I retreat to the far coast to stay out of sight. Who is he, and what does he want?

The adventurer slings a bag over one shoulder and, with a walking stick in hand, sets out across the heath. The wind tumbles as fierce as ever, but I can hear the man whistling as he strides across the peat moss and rocks. His first destination is the old kirk ruins. He explores each turn of its labyrinthine walls and stone architecture. Emerging from a doorway, he produces a small notebook, and drops to one knee to scribble in it. Moving further away, he drops again to sketch the exterior of the ruins from a different angle. Minutes later, the notebook slips back into his pocket, and he resumes his reconnaissance.

Who is this traveler? He is too far away for me to make out his features, but his bearing speaks volumes. Chin up and chest out, he marches forward with a proud step like one who seldom finds his path blocked. A product of wealth and class, I presume. Perhaps he is the current laird of the island, newly inherited from his father. How long have I been on this blasted rock? I do not remember. Maybe I have always been here, since before the time of the Norsemen. I am the ghost of Eynhallow, am I not?

I watch the explorer enter the abandoned cottage nearest to the ruins. What was the name of the people who lived here? Dearness, yes, that's it. Something and somebody Dearness. The newcomer enters the building for a time before returning to the sunshine. He stops to take notes before resuming his hike to the next croft in the distance.

Again, my memory fails to recall the family that lived here. I remember not liking them, but the reasons for my enmity are as foggy as their names. The adventurer explores this cottage briefly, and then he's off again. I lurch after him at a safe distance.

The third croft he explores stirs a harder memory in my muddled brain. My friend lived here long ago. Something terrible was done to her after death. Before I can scratch up the errant details, the explorer resumes his hike. His destination lies uphill to the one stone cottage where I never go. Watching him enter, a snippet of memory bobs to the surface. This was my home. The place where my children were born and where I raised them before something terrible happened. How long has it been now? I have lost all track of time. My children's names come back to me like a hammer striking an anvil. Grace and Kit and Meg and little Euphemia. In that order. Whatever happened to them? I wonder where they are now and if they are happy. I wonder how old each of them would be, but I cannot fathom a guess since time has lost all meaning. Ten years? Twenty? More?

Oh God.

The gentleman with the noble bearing reappears to scribble in his notebook before resuming his hike. He looks pleased and engaged like he is on some great quest. Or pilgrimage, maybe. This is holy isle after all, is it not? I don't know. I have never seen God in this place and I of all creatures should recognize the divine when I see it. Not that I am pious, mind you. I exist in a clammy limbo between life and death, and yet, never have I felt anything holy here. There is rock and water and salt, nothing more.

Twice he stops to turn and scan the landscape behind him. He has ears, this one. They detect my shuffling gait. The explorer shrugs and carries on.

The pathway to the last farm is all but overgrown by now. This cottage is another that I do not visit or ever seek shelter in. It is haunted, I recall now. So much is flooding back as I observe the stranger tour through the abandoned homes. Things I want to remember, but also things I do not. That is the curse of memory, I suppose. The walls of this particular croft are black with soot, the roof timbers scorched raw. There was a fire here. Did I start it? I believe I did. Why?

The stranger lingers inside for too long. I creep up to the blasted window and peer inside. The man sifts through the rubbish and debris of the cottage. He lifts strange-looking instruments from the ground and brushes the grit away. He sketches a number of these odd artifacts before sifting the ashy sand with a trowel for more. Broken glass is unearthed, along with metal gears and rusty surgeon's knives. The man delights in each find, placing his treasures on a length of cloth he has unfurled before resuming his dig. Tugging another treasure from the grit, he hoots with laughter. In his hands is the remains of a notebook, singed along one side from the fire. Setting this aside gently, he digs on and on, uncovering a second scorched notebook.

Shadows deepen as the sun sinks into the sea. I watch the man gather up his artifacts and leave the inhospitable shelter of the roofless structure. It had a name once. Merryman, that's it. The explorer leaves, retreating downhill to the cottage I used to call home. It still has a roof and a door to block out the never-ending wind. I watch him tumble wood into the hearth to get the fire started. From his sack, he unfurls a blanket on the floor for a bed. A cloth bundle is unwrapped to reveal a dinner of cheese, dry sausage, and a few pieces of dark bread. He nibbles on this as he gingerly turns the pages of the unearthed notebooks before the light of the fire.

I study the man for a good while. Something about his features tugs at loose threads of memory, but nothing solid enough for me to get a clean grip on. There is no possible way I could have met this man before, and yet that face suggests strange familiarity. Could it possibly be my son? I had a son—I am sure of it. Christopher. No, Kit. Is this lone adventurer him, returned to the place of his birth after all this time?

I watch and wait. The embers pulse weakly in the hearth and the man finally sets the notebooks aside. He stretches out on the bedroll before the fire, using his satchel as a pillow. I maintain my vigil for a while yet. I want a closer look, but do not want to alarm the adventurer.

Graceful is something I am not. I lurch to the front door, trying to be as silent as a house cat. I try to remember why my left leg is so absurdly bent, but the cause of its deformity remains a mystery. The heavy door hangs from its hinges. I lift it to prevent the wood from scraping loudly against the floor. A closer look at the man's face is all I want, a quick study that might unravel this nagging shred of memory for me.

The prone figure sits up. I turn to stone.

"Hello," he says. "I had a feeling I was being watched."

My thoughts shatter like eggs dropped to the floor, and I cannot decide on a course of action. Do I flee or stay? Oddly, the explorer is neither shocked nor alarmed by my intrusion. He smiles like we are old friends. Instead, I am the one who is struck dumb.

"Come, come," he bids me, waving me in. "Let me stir the fire to life and we shall talk."

A low growl issues across the room. I am startled to find the source of this sound is me. It has been so long since I have spoken that my throat has rusted shut.

The man rises to his feet and stands very straight, very formal. He bows in greeting.

"How do you do," he says. "I am Hugo Frankenstein."

CHAPTER XLIV

He smiles and again motions for me to sit as he adds a broken table leg to the fire. His welcome knocks me off balance. Do people not shriek in fright at my appearance? Am I misremembering this?

"I have heard stories about this place being haunted," he says, banking the embers against the new wood. "On the mainland, they tell stories about the ghost of Eynhallow."

He turns back to me, but I have not moved from the doorway. His eyes narrow. "Do you not speak? Come closer, please. Where I can see you better."

My tattered cloak drags along the floor. The rekindled fire throws more light to the man's face. The lofty brow, the intense eyes and shape of the mouth. I see it now, the resemblance to Victor.

The name has been lost for so long, but it pops to the surface like a cork in a pond. Victor Frankenstein. He loved me once, didn't he? My throat constricts as I try to push words out but all that comes is a gruesome croaking noise. I close my mouth.

The man stands the poker against the stone and brushes his hands. "My father was Ernest Frankenstein. Not that you would know him, of course. He was an honest man. Uncomplicated. He was also the only surviving member of his family. Within the span of two years, the whole lot of them were struck down. My grandfather, two uncles, and a half-cousin. A lot of death in a short time. My father always suspected it had something to do with his brother, Victor, but it was only a suspicion. He rarely spoke of the man."

The visitor roots around in his satchel and brings forth a few items wrapped in cloth. More cheese, a few biscuits. "Are you hungry? I can't imagine what you scavenge for food in this place. It's a bit desolate, isn't it?"

Neither the sight nor the smell of the food stirs me. I have not felt hunger in a long time. My eyes are hungry, after a fashion. I cannot stop staring at this stranger. Not so much a stranger now, I suppose. Victor's nephew.

Eynhallow

"You are staggeringly tall, aren't you?" He looks up at me with something akin to wonder. He pulls up the stool and again, motions for me to take the chair. "Please, sit. I will ruin my neck if I must crane it up at you."

My bones crack like dry wood as I sit. Almost eye level now, but I still look down on him.

"My father passed two years ago," he says, "leaving me the heir to the name Frankenstein and its various titles. But that's all it was, you see. A creaky old title, but little wealth or property. Our family has been much reduced in status and fortune since the days of Victor. As a result, there wasn't much to inherit in the way of assets, but there were a great number of papers and books. The letters and writings of my uncle, Victor. I pored through them and discovered so many strange things. The man's work, his life. The many correspondences from his father and fiancée. Along with his journals. My God, the man's journals. I was fascinated by it all. Nay, I became obsessed."

There is a knife in his hand. He cuts a wedge of cheese and pops it into his mouth.

"You can imagine my shock at reading of his accomplishments. I never met the man, you see, so I had nothing to go on save for these journals. Was Victor some madman who dreamed up all these fantastical notions, or had he actually achieved them? The creation of life from dead tissue? Good God. It is the very primal spark of the universe that he found. In fact, how did he put it?" He snaps his fingers to stir his memory. "Oh, yes—*I have lifted the skirts of Mother Nature and glimpsed her secrets*. Ha! Can you imagine?"

Another slice of cheese. He chews with his mouth open.

"I needed to know the truth, you see, so I set out to uncover it. I have spent the last year, along with a fair sum of money, retracing the steps of Victor Frankenstein. To piece together the clues and find tangible evidence of his great achievements. Which has led me here, to this place where, according to his journals, he was to forge a mate for his fiendish creation. Although, his records are unclear on whether he accomplished this task. He claims to have had second thoughts and abandoned the project before completion. And yet here you are."

The memories are shards of broken glass. They twinkle with discombobulated bits of images and harsh voices. A flash of this or that, but not enough to reflect the whole. Some are dull, while others are sharp enough to cut clean to the bone. My flesh recalls the painful jolt of resurrection. Or the cold fingers of the sea as my cadaver was thrown overboard. My hands ripping an ear from a misshapen head.

He's still talking, this Hugo Frankenstein. He is on his feet, pacing and making gestures much like his late uncle. Family traits, I assume.

"I am astonished that you exist," he says, clapping his palms together. "That you have survived after all this time! I have learned nothing of the fate of the creature. He supposedly wandered into the arctic wasteland, never to be seen again. And yet how can this be verified? It cannot. But you, my lovely. You are as real as rain."

My tongue grits like sand, my lips crack and split. My throat is seized, the vocal cords corroded by lack of use. It takes great effort to force out the first words spoken in a long time. But how long?

"What…year?"

Now he startles. "You can speak! I wasn't sure if you were mute or just witless." The man leans close, scrutinizing my face, my mouth. "It did occur to me that whatever was done to you might have sizzled your brains into soup. I am glad it did not."

I seize his wrist, wordlessly demanding an answer.

"Yes, the year. It is eighteen thirty-nine. June, to be precise."

The figure makes no sense to me. A random number without context. How old are my children? All adults by now, perhaps parents or even grandparents. Are they still alive? Are they happy? Little Effie would be fourscore years and then some. Does she remember me as I was or does she only recall the pallid ghost she encountered in the ruins? Perhaps she doesn't think of me at all.

This man enjoys the sound of his own voice. I shake off my musty thoughts as he continues to pace and orate like some petty laird. He is prattling on about glory and genius now.

"For too long, my uncle's achievements have been hidden from sight, but no more." He retrieves the burnt notebook excavated from the ash. "This proves it, as does your existence. The name of Victor Frankenstein will be exalted to the highest glory. His superior intellect and his bravery will astonish the world. I will publish papers about him so that all will know what a noble hero he was. How he had stolen fire from the gods and brought it to us mere mortals."

I am on my feet, towering over this man Frankenstein. He stops, looks at me with a puzzled face. "You will be a part of that legacy. You are the proof of his great achievements."

"Victor…was…" How raw my voice is. How excruciating it is to push each syllable from my mouth.

The man is quivering with anticipation. "Yes, yes. Victor was what? Brilliant? Genius? Heroic? Tell me."

"…scum."

His face falls. This is not the reply he expects or wants. He objects to my slander, but his protest is clipped short by my hand around his throat. His eyes, as russet as an October leaf, bulge from their sockets and the tongue oozes grotesquely from his mouth. His neck snaps. The body flops to the ground like a sack of mealy corn.

I return to the chair and sit for a long time with the dead man at my feet. The night leeches into gray, and then a bright gold paints the undersides of the clouds as the sun rises. I break up the wooden stool and feed it to the fire. Frankenstein lies on the floor, his plain brown eyes now crimson with bloodshot. His little cheese knife lays near his head. I take it up and saw through the shirt and vest before cutting deep into his chest. My fingers wriggle inside and crack apart the ribs to get at the heart. It plucks free with a wet sucking noise. I pierce it on the iron skewer and turn it slowly over the fire until it hisses and steams. I have not felt hunger in a long time, but I am ravenous now. The ruby meat chars and blackens over the flames and when it is roasted, I eat it.

The rest of him rots. The gulls smell it and come pecking and then the worms come to wriggle in the putrid flesh. One more turn of the seasons and he is bone and dried flaps of leather. His skull sits in the corner, limed with gull droppings.

His boat remains on the shore, battered by the weather. It breaks apart easily and I throw the pieces into the surf. More seasons cycle through and another boat beaches on the shore. I retreat to the cliff and watch the landing party move about the island. The men from the mainland light torches and burn the dry thatch roofs of every croft, rendering them unfit for dwelling. The arsonists climb back into their boat and row away, leaving the ghost in peace.

No one comes to Eynhallow anymore.

Visits to Eynhallow island are limited to one day of the year, typically in July. Trips can be arranged through the Orkney Heritage Society.

ACKNOWLEDGMENTS

The first acknowledgment goes to the mother of horror herself, Mary Shelley. Can you believe she was only 18 years old when she wrote the first and greatest myth of the modern era? It's hard to think of anything more iconic or metaphorical than the name Frankenstein.

Huge thanks to Jennifer Barnes of Raw Dog Screaming Press, who shepherded this book through to completion. Like all great editors, Jennifer asked critical questions and encouraged me to go too far. Thanks also to Adam Pitts for his keen eye.

Special thanks to Catherine McCarthy, author extraordinaire and good friend, whose feedback on early drafts was invaluable. Thanks also to author Coy Hall, whose expertise helped make this shine.

Always, always thanks to Monique for her love and support. Buckets of love and appreciation to Ginger and Ruby because you two are awesome! To Mom, forever.

Thanks also to Chris and Jason Krawczyk. Not just for having the best book shop ever, but for being pals and letting me hang out with you. Love you guys!

I also want to salute Elsa Lanchester who portrayed both Mary Shelley and the monster's intended in the 1935 classic, *The Bride of Frankenstein*. Lanchester's portrayal of the lightning haired bride only runs to about five minutes of actual screen time, but she created a true horror icon that seared itself into my young impressionable brain. Thanks, Elsa!

Content Warnings: Violence, spousal abuse, childbirth trauma, animal death, infant death, cannibalism, graphic imagery

ABOUT THE AUTHOR

Tim McGregor is the author of *Wasps in the Ice Cream, Taboo in Four Colors*, the Shirley Jackson Award-nominated *Lure*, and *Hearts Strange and Dreadful*. A former screenwriter and current HWA member, Tim lives in Toronto with his wife, two kids, and one spiteful ghost. He can be reached at timmcgregorauthor.com

Printed in the USA
CPSIA information can be obtained
at www.ICGtesting.com
LVHW040526020224
770666LV00002BA/12